Island

A Wastelander Novella

E.S. Luck

Sleepwalker Books

Cover design by: GetCovers

Contents

Content Note

Island is a post-apocalyptic romance that takes place in a world where violence is a daily reality. As such, please read the following content note carefully and take extra care if you may find its setting, themes, or events distressing. Readers can expect graphic violence, death, cannibalism, miscarriage (mentioned only), alcohol consumption (mild), and scenes of explicit sexual intimacy (all among consenting adults).

Pronunciation Guide

Isla - *EYE-lah.*

Oisín - *Oh-SHEEN.* Irish language equivalent of Owen.

Aoife - *EE-fuh.* Irish language name often anglicized as Eva, though it has no true English equivalent.

Chapter 1
Noah

June 2093

No man is an island. Take one part of the whole away and we all suffer. Take away billions of people, and there's hardly anything left to cling to. Of course, that all happened before I was even born. The only world I know is this one, where former cities are now ruins, where wilderness overtakes all it touches, and where I scavenge through the wreckage that was once a world for whatever I can find to keep my tiny island of humanity alive.

"Noah!" Isla trilled, some thirty paces ahead of me in the woods. "You're missing out!"

"On what, kitten?" I called back, unable to hold back a smile. "More trees? A bird? Haven't even seen deer today, and the way you're hollering, we won't."

Isla jogged back to me, her pretty blonde ponytail whipping over her shoulders. Her deep blue eyes sparkled with mischief as usual.

"Hardly matters since we're not here for deer," she said. "I found what might be a big score for PNCs."

PNCs. Portable Universal Nano Controllers. The small, blue, crystalline parts that made all the electronics of the Old World work. Nowadays, they were priceless for those of us living in the Valley. The place had a real name once, but hardly anybody remembered it—only the ones who'd lived there before the virus destroyed everything, and there weren't too many of them left now. It was the only safe place around for miles, mostly because it was a secret. Only we knew it existed, and we didn't take in outsiders. After all, when the rest of the world was merely eking out an existence in the ruins of the Old World, everyone wanted what we had. Our safety lay in secrecy.

PNCs were why we had electricity and running water when nobody else did. Why we were able to farm on a much larger scale than anywhere else. Why we'd always had food, shelter, and basic medical care. We worked damn hard to keep it all going, but we had more than most. I'd heard rumours about big, walled-in compounds where they had even more, but you didn't look for them. Not unless you had a death wish.

"So that's what you dragged me out here for?" I asked. "And here I thought you just wanted some alone time."

Isla laughed. "You wish."

My chest ached. I did.

"I needed someone to watch my back," she continued with a bright smile that broke my heart. "And I heard you're the guy for that. Plus, you needed to get out of that cabin. You've been cooped up by yourself lately, and I missed you."

I grunted noncommittally, but my heart leaped at the idea that she'd been missing me. Even knowing how stupid it was. Even knowing that there was no way I could have her.

"You done buttering me up yet?" I asked. "How dangerous is this gonna be?"

She shrugged, giving me that coy smile that always turned my legs to jelly. She'd been my best friend my whole life, and I still wasn't totally used to my response to her. I didn't know if I'd ever be.

"No idea," Isla answered. "But it's not like that ever stopped us before."

"Stopped *you* before," I corrected.

She rolled her eyes. "Yeah, yeah, you're the one always keeping me from getting myself killed; I've heard this speech a million times. Can we skip it this time?"

"Just this once," I agreed, dodging a low-hanging branch. "What makes you think this place is gonna have PNCs?"

"The cellar door looks untouched, and old, as in, before the Fall," Isla said, chewing her lip. "It's behind some rubble, but the lock was intact. I was scavving for something else, so no bolt cutters, and I'm not sure my dainty girl hands could've cut it myself anyway."

She held up her hands, dirty and callused from hard work and grinned at me.

"That's why I needed a massive, bearded bear of a man to help me."

I rolled my eyes, but I was impressed. An untouched cellar might mean an intact electrical box.

"Come on, big guy," she said, gesturing for me to hurry up. "We want to be back before nightfall."

The forest stretched on for a long time, but eventually gave way to a village...or what was left of it. Didn't look like much now. There was a single street of houses and small shops, but all were overgrown, their structures crumbling after twenty-five years of neglect. Exposed brick and rebar stuck out everywhere, and vines worked through the holes in the buildings. Ivy covered every surface. In a life after the apocalypse, you got to know that slowly but surely, nature always crept in and reclaimed everything. Always a matter of when, not if.

Isla walked to the end of the cracked, broken remains of the street and stopped in front of the remains of a house that was fixing to fall down. Under a pile of rubble, I could just make out the outline of a cellar door.

"Good work, kitten," I said, and she preened.

PNCs were always a big deal. They'd been getting harder and harder to find lately. Oisín seemed to think that we needed to go farther out, but no one wanted to risk that. He warned that we'd run out in just a few years, but he'd been overruled by the others. It was too dangerous, and besides, they'd argued, we could ration them if the situation got worse.

I didn't know that I agreed, but I sure as hell wasn't going out there, and I reckoned anyone who would was crazier than a shot at rat, as my Pop liked to say.

"See any totems?" I asked, and Isla shook her head.

"I didn't have time to look," she answered. "But let's do a sweep now. I don't like how bold the maneaters have been getting. Or how they've multiplied."

We searched the area, looking for signs of cannibals—primitive, feral humans that'd reverted to what my Pop called their lizard brains. They hunted in packs, dressed in rags and the remains of their victims. Once upon a time, they'd been people, according to Ma, but over the generation or two since the fall, they'd been breeding, and the offspring raised on eating human flesh had pretty much lost their humanity. Something about eating people screws you in the head, I guess. Who could've predicted that?

As I passed a collapsed half of a wall, something metallic caught the sunlight. I turned. It was a dog tag...hung around what was once a human head. I would've been surprised I didn't smell it first, but since it was summer, the flesh was all dried out in the sun. The jawbone was missing, and hollowed eye sockets stared at nothing. Not even the crows would want this now.

"Damn," Isla said from behind me. "I was hoping we wouldn't find any."

I went to examine closer. "Looks old. Like it's been here a spell."

She nodded. "Let's risk it, then."

I rolled my eyes. She was always the one who wanted to run headfirst into danger. She was a brave little thing, and I liked that about her, but good grief, a little caution never killed anyone.

Isla saw my expression and added defensively, "We'll be in the cellar anyway; no one will see us until we leave. C'mon. We need this, especially if what Oisín said is true."

I sighed. "Alright. But you gotta keep watch. Anything fishy, and we split. No complaints."

She agreed, so we walked back to the pile of rubble covering the cellar door. Together, we shifted the rocks to get access. The hinges squealed as I lifted the heavy metal door, and we both winced. Isla kept watch through a crack in the door. Flashlight and bolt cutters out, I started down the cracked concrete steps. At the bottom, I was hit with a damp, mouldy smell. *Shit.* I hoped that the PNCs weren't destroyed by moisture.

There was water all over, gathered in puddles wherever the floor dipped. Mud seeped in through cracks in the foundation, sucking on my boots as I walked. The cellar was one room, with a rotted wood door that must've once led upstairs hanging off its hinges. Only rubble lay behind it. I crossed to the far side, where my flashlight finally illuminated a small metal box on the wall, secured with a rusted padlock.

"Looks good," I called back to Isla. "Untouched."

"Really? That's awesome! Now hurry up, this place reeks."

Amused, I cut through the lock without much effort. Inside, there was a complex electronic housing that might have been used for anything back before the Fall and sure enough, there they were: ten small blue crystals, mounted in the electronics. I carefully started to remove the first one.

"Noah!" Isla called, and there was a note of concern in her voice. "We're not alone."

I heard the swish of her bow, and a shriek of pain from outside. Maneaters.

I hurried as much as I could, but detaching each of the small crystals without damaging them took time—too much time. I heard more shrieks of pain, and glanced over my shoulder to see Isla firing off arrows almost as fast as she could draw them.

"They're too close!" she said, frazzled, and backed further into the cellar, bow still drawn. "Get ready!"

I only had two crystals left. There was no time. I grabbed the box and heaved, yanking it off the decaying wall.

The distinct shrieks of cannibals filled the cellar, and Isla screamed. I whirled back to her. She'd hit another with an arrow and had her knife out. She held her own, slashing and stabbing like a fierce little warrior, but there were too many for her to take on her own.

I unholstered my pistol and shot a couple of cannibals by the cellar door. The others were too close to Isla.

"Noah!" she cried out.

One had grabbed her by the throat. He slammed her against the wall, trying to get in close and tear at her flesh with broken, jagged teeth. I charged and brought the bolt cutters down on his head with all my strength. He staggered, then dropped like a stone. With her out of immediate danger, I took a position in front of Isla and fought the rest of the maneaters until the last one tried to run, only to catch a bullet in the back. My Pop always said, if you let one maneater get away, they'll be back with a dozen before you know it.

We packed up the precious PNC's, and started the long walk home.

***

Several hours later, back in the Valley, we could finally relax...sort of. Minutes later, thunder crashed, and I threw a worried look at the sky. Dark clouds had rolled in, and it was fixing to storm any minute, I was sure of it. The air had gotten thick, and that charged, still silence that always came before a storm had set in.

"We're not gonna make it," Isla said, giving the sky a worried glance.

I was thinking the same. We always went on scav runs with a tent packed for just this kind of scenario, but the thought of sleeping outside in a downpour didn't appeal. But when thunder rumbled, and a raindrop hit my cheek, there wasn't much choice.

We found a clearing and set up the tent, far from any trees. Just as we finished, the downpour began. Isla laughed and scrambled into the tent, me on her heels. We rolled out our sleeping bags and laid down. I retrieved a thin book from my pack, then reclined against it, using the pack as a pillow.

"Don't tell me we're *reading*," Isla groaned, and I scoffed. "Talk to me instead."

I rolled my eyes. "You have the attention span of a horse in heat."

"To be fair, mares in heat are very focused. Just on the one thing, though."

A smile tugged at my lips, but I still cracked open my book to read. Isla gave me a grand total of two minutes of silence before she said, "Whatcha reading?"

I showed her the faded cover of *Southern Desserts: Iconic and Delicious Recipes,* then flipped to the chapter about cobbler. It was one of the only books stashed in my parents' attic, and I'd found it as a teenager under a box of old clothes. The spine was cracked now; I'd read it dozens of times.

She grinned and moved closer to me on our side-by-side sleeping bags. The heat of her sent goosebumps up my arm. I wanted to touch her. Even though I knew I couldn't. Even though I knew she wouldn't want that.

"Who knew that big, gruff Noah Harding's deep, dark secret was a love of dainty pastries," she teased. "I doubt anyone, at a glance, would suspect a thing. Why do you keep reading a cookbook, though?"

I thought for a minute.

"Makes me feel connected to whatever heritage I have," I finally answered. "Recipes from where my Ma and Pop came from."

"The States?"

"Yeah. Doesn't make much sense, but it kinda makes me feel nostalgic."

"Nostalgic?" Isla said with a smile. "For a time and place you never had?"

I swallowed. "Yeah. I guess so."

Ma and Pop were originally from the South, though they didn't talk about it much. Hard to mistake them for anything else when they opened their mouths, though. They moved up to Northern Ontario, to the Valley, a year or two before things got really bad with the virus and the world went to hell. I was lucky they hadn't stayed, because rumour had it that things had been even worse down south, but...I had a yearning for this place and this past that I'd never been part of, but somehow still held a connection to.

Someone had to remember it. If I didn't, who would?

"I brought something to eat," I said, grabbing my pack and rummaging through it. "Since we're stuck here for a while."

"Oh, good," Isla replied. "I'm starving."

I'd wrapped up two leftover slices of my sweet potato pie. I took one for myself and handed the other to her.

"Oh my God," Isla moaned as she bit into it. "It's amazing. Like always."

I tried to hide how happy that made me, but she must've seen a small smile tug at my lips, because she leaned closer to me.

"If you were stranded on a desert island, what three things would you bring?" Isla said, a playful grin on her face.

I set down the book.

"Dunno," I said, more interested in her answer. "What would *you* bring?"

"Cop out," she teased, then bit her lip thoughtfully. "My bow. Water. And my crochet basket."

I snorted. "Crochet?"

She smacked my arm playfully. "Yeah! In case I get bored, obviously. And what would Mr. I-Don't-Know bring?"

"Water and a loaded rifle."

"That's only two things, big guy."

I looked over at her pretty, peaches-and-cream complexion, her blond hair falling like a curtain over her shoulder. Her blue eyes were always bright, teasing, beautiful. How many times had I lain with her just like this—on countless sleepovers, on long summer days in the grass? Shooting the breeze, laughing together. She was the only one who really made me laugh on a regular basis.

Probably because everyone else thinks you're basically mute, I told myself grimly. Isla was the only one who really knew me, who understood me, because she'd known me forever and, unlike the rest of the Valley, took the time to coax me out of my shell.

"You," I said, looking over into her eyes. "Couldn't go to a deserted place without my right-hand, could I?"

Something in her eyes softened, and she moved even closer to me. I couldn't help but notice the pretty S-curve of her body, the full curve of her breasts under her shirt, and the scent of her skin. I wanted to kiss her, but I couldn't. It'd gone all wrong last time.

"I'm your desert island girl?"

I chuckled, a little nervously. "Sure you are, kitten."

Her face was only a couple inches from mine now, and the cute freckles on her nose stood out. I couldn't help myself—she was too close. I reached over and pushed a stray lock of golden hair out of her face.

She reacted like my touch burned her, starting and moving back, letting out a long breath. *You're so stupid,* I said to myself, irritated by my slip. *She doesn't want you like that.*

"Can't believe you still call me that, after all these years," Isla said with a half-hearted laugh. "Kitty's ten years old now."

I shrugged. "How could I not, seeing how you cried over her?"

Isla smiled, a little wistfully. "She was so little, with her tiny, twisted front legs."

Ten years before, one of the barn cats had a litter of kittens at the McNeils' farm. The smallest and weakest of them had deformed front legs. She could walk, but it was more of a hobble than anything. Not much use as a barn cat.

"And then Dad said he was going to put her down," she continued with a sigh.

"You cried like a baby," I said, smiling slightly at the memory. "Still remember how you begged him to let you keep her. Promised you'd take care of her totally on your own, at nine years old."

"And I did!" Isla retorted. "She's had a better life than probably 90% of cats."

"Better than 99%, I'd say," I said, and it was true. Kitty was a queen among cats, mostly living out her days on Isla's bed on her very own crocheted pillow. "Could've thought of a better name, though."

"I was nine! And not very creative."

I snorted. "And you've been kitten to me ever since, so the nickname matches your creativity level."

We passed a couple minutes in silence, and as she finished her last bite of pie, Isla's smile slowly changed to something else that I couldn't read.

"Noah," she said cautiously, "why haven't you been around as much lately? I don't know, maybe I'm imagining it, but for the past few months, ever since I—"

"It's nothing," I cut in bluntly. "It's nothing to do with you. Just my own stuff, like usual. Haven't felt like being out and about with people."

It was only partly true. It was also getting harder and harder to be around someone I wanted so badly but knew I couldn't have. Especially after our kiss last year, which neither of us seemed to be able to talk about.

It'd been her nineteenth birthday. We'd taken one of the old forest trails in the Valley on horseback to a small clearing, just as night was falling. Under the stars, we kissed...and that was it.

It was the most perfect moment of my life, her soft lips pressed to mine, my hand in her hair. It was what I'd waited for, for what felt like forever. And then somehow, it'd gone all wrong. Things were awkward between us after, and that's when I'd found out that she'd started seeing him. And that she didn't want me. Not like that.

Isla's blue eyes darted over the last bit of my pie in my hand, before she quickly looked away. I sighed.

"Here," I said, holding it out to her. "You have it."

"But—"

"It's fine, kitten. You look hungry."

She swallowed, then nodded. "Thank you."

She reached over to take the pie, and our fingers touched. The warmth of her hand teased me with everything I couldn't have, and our eyes met briefly. She cleared her throat and looked away as she took the pie. We sat in silence as she ate.

After she finished, she stretched out on her sleeping bag, her eyelids fluttering. I laid down beside her, feeling tired myself. It'd been a long day, and the rain pattering on the tent was vaguely soothing.

"You shouldn't be all by yourself so much," Isla said with a yawn. "You're coming to the dance tomorrow, right?"

Ugh. I'd been trying to forget it. Every month, we had a council meeting in the Valley to discuss community matters, and afterwards, there was a dance. Lots of people looked forward to it, but I never did. It was just another opportunity for me to be the quiet guy who didn't know how to talk to anyone. Being the tallest, biggest guy in any given room didn't help my image as the strong, silent type either.

Seeing my expression, Isla touched my hand, sending more tingles up my arm.

"C'mon," she pleaded. "Everyone wants to see you. I know John and Kimmy will."

I scoffed, and she tried again: "Please, Noah. It's not good for you to be holed up in that cabin all the time. I miss you."

I sighed. I couldn't say no to her. She was still my best friend. And I wasn't strong enough to stay away.

"Alright. But just for you."

She grinned. "Sarah's bringing her famous honey cakes."

"Okay, maybe a little for that, too."

Chapter 2
Noah

The council meeting the next day passed without incident at the Lodge, the big hall that served as our community hub. Oisín gave yet another speech about the importance of widening our net to search for PNCs, and as usual, Jameson and his people dissented, and there was a whole 'nother debate on before we knew it. I'd already heard a couple versions of this argument—we all had—so I passed the time by watching Isla, who sat next to me. The dance afterward was one of our only opportunities to dress up, and she'd worn a knee-length blue dress that matched her eyes and hugged her curves. Her long, golden blonde hair was swept over her shoulder. She'd gotten even prettier over the last couple years, which only made it harder to pretend I hadn't noticed.

Finally, the meeting ended with a congratulations to Emilia and Leon on their recent marriage. I hadn't gone to the wedding even though I'd been invited, like everyone else in the Valley. I just wasn't good at this kind of thing. I hated crowds, and I'd rather be on my own than talk to people I only knew in passing. Besides, I always had plenty of work to do at Brookside. Isla had begged me to go, but when I refused, she left early from the reception and went fishing with me instead.

We stood from our chairs and started moving them to make room for the dance. Once the floor had been cleared, I headed back to meet Isla, but a certain tall, dark-haired guy beat me to her. John had a unique look that stood out in the crowd, if only because of his weird hair, which was dark brown and shoulder-length with shaved sides. No idea why he thought that was a good look, but clearly it didn't stop him from getting girls, because Isla arched up and kissed him.

"John," I said in greeting, trying not to sound too resentful.

"Hey, buddy, long time, no see," he answered with a smile that even I could admit was charming. "Isla tells me you've been MIA lately. You should have a drink with us."

I nodded but didn't say anything. I'd known John my whole life, just like almost everyone here, and up until he started dating my best friend, I'd probably have called him a friend, too. His grandparents, Oisín and Aoife, were long-time friends of Ma and Pop.

It was just hard now, seeing him get to touch her. And with his stupid hair and stupid smile and goddamn *likable* personality, he could've had anyone he wanted. Why did he have to pick the only girl that *I* wanted? Judging by the pointed glances that several of the single women in this room were giving him, he could've had his pick.

My jealous brooding was interrupted by John's sister, Kimmy, appearing at his opposite side. She was short and petite, her black hair tied up in a bun, and if I didn't know better, I'd have described her as dainty...except I'd once seen her stab a maneater in the eye with a blade she'd kept hidden in her shirt, then pull it out and cut its throat, quickly and efficiently, like she was carving a Sunday roast.

"Hi, Noah," she said cheerfully to me, and I grunted in acknowledgement. "How's your mom feeling? Is that salve working well on her fingers?"

Ma had arthritis now, and she'd gone to Aoife for help. Kimmy worked as her apprentice to provide basic medical care for the Valley. Sometimes there wasn't much they could do for major ailments, since we didn't have much Old World equipment, but they did their best with what they had.

"Yeah," I replied. "Thanks."

There was an awkward silence caused by my inability to just talk like a normal person, but thankfully, Kimmy was the type that could blow right past that.

"Come sit with us," she said, gesturing towards a group of chairs at the edge of the room. "They'll be starting the music soon."

Isla shot me a look that said *please do this for me,* so I sighed and followed the three of them over to the chairs, where a glass of whiskey was eventually pressed into my hands, courtesy of the Madigans. They made all kinds of drink at their homestead, Summerhurst, but whiskey was their specialty. Aoife was there, and she greeted me with her usual enthusiasm. It wasn't hard to see where Kimmy got her personality.

A small band set up to play, and soon, music and dancing was in full swing.

"Don't you just love them?" Isla gushed, nodding at Emilia and Leon, who were dancing near us. "They're so cute. I hope our wedding is as beautiful as theirs was."

There was a heavy silence where both Kimmy and John suddenly looked incredibly uncomfortable. Sadly, I wasn't the right person to break the tension with a joke, so it just hung there for a minute until John stood abruptly and walked over to Isla's older brother, Danny, who was standing in the opposite corner of the hall with a drink in his hand. Isla stared after him, the beginnings of hurt on her face, and I had to force myself not to touch her.

"Isla, come dance with me," Kimmy said as she stood, holding out her hands with a forced smile.

Isla gave her a confused look but allowed herself to be led onto the dance floor. I watched them go, sipping on my drink idly. Other people came up and tried to make small talk with me, which was painful, but I managed to get through it. When the song ended, Isla stood in the middle of the dance floor with Kimmy, who was talking rapidly to her in a low voice. Her expression made me haul myself up; she looked like she might be about to cry.

"What's up?" I said as I arrived at Isla's side.

"Nothing," Kimmy said smoothly. "Just girl talk, but I better go check on Granny."

She turned and walked back over to our chairs, where Aoife was suddenly nowhere to be found.

Isla shook her head. "It's nothing, Noah. I want to go home."

I raised my eyebrows. "But you love these stupid things."

That, at least, made her laugh. She looked back over to where Kimmy was waiting for her grandmother, who was being led back over to a chair by her husband.

"Aoife, darling, you work too hard," Oisín was saying to his wife in his mild Irish brogue as he led her by the hand. "At the clinic all day today and yesterday. You're not twenty-one anymore, my love, and you haven't been well lately. Time for you to relax."

He slapped a kiss against her cheek as she sank into her chair, then gestured at Kimmy.

"Kimmy, love, get your grandmother a whiskey."

The small Irishwoman scoffed. "I'm grand, dear. I can damn well get my own whiskey."

"Of course you can, Granny," Kimmy said indulgently. "But why would you, when your favourite grandchild can do it for you?"

Aoife rolled her eyes but couldn't hide a smile. "Thank you, dearest."

While Kimmy went to fetch the whiskey, Oisín kept his hands on Aoife's shoulders, gently kneading. She leaned her head back against him, looking weary, and he brushed a tendril of silver hair out of her face.

Isla sighed. "Someday, I want that."

"Want what?" I asked, my eyes moving to her wistful expression.

She looked up at me with something like sadness.

"To be wanted," she answered. "To be loved so deeply that my husband still takes care of me when I'm old. And to have children—grandchildren—that close to me."

A knot tightened in my chest. "Don't worry. You will."

"How do you know?"

"People like you don't end up alone," I answered.

People like me do, I stopped myself from saying. The truth was, I didn't mind that most of the time...but seeing the Madigans was always a reminder that, whatever I may've felt about John dating Isla, we were stronger together. And I wanted that for Isla, in the end...even if it wasn't with me.

Kimmy returned to Aoife's side with a cup of whiskey, and Aoife took it gratefully.

"Speaking of our lesser grandchildren," Oisín said to Kimmy with a wry grin, "where's that boy of ours gotten to?"

She laughed. "I'll find him."

Isla's gaze hadn't moved from Oisín and Aoife, and the corners of her mouth had turned down.

"What's bothering you, kitten?" I said softly.

She sighed. "Want to get another drink? I need one."

"Alright," I said with a nod. "But then you have to tell me."

We went to the drink table and poured a couple more, but she barely touched hers. She stared at the amber liquid in the glass like it was going to tell her the solution to all her problems.

Just when I was about to prompt her again about whatever was bothering her, she said, "Dance with me, Noah."

I studied her. She looked slightly tipsy.

Hesitating, I said, "Doesn't John want to dance with you?"

She grinned. "Nah. He's not much of a dancer. Not sure anyone could drag his ass out here. He and Danny are busy talking each other's ears off, anyway."

I looked at them, standing in the corner. John spoke to Danny in a low, serious voice. Danny listened intently, nodding along...and neither of them even glanced in our direction.

"C'mon," Isla prompted, holding out her hand. "You're much better at this than I am, and I need someone to make me look good."

I suppressed a smile. "Don't think you need any help in that area. You're real pretty tonight, kitten."

To my surprise, she flushed a little, smiling sweetly. I took her hand and drew her closer to me, my other hand on her waist. Her hand felt small in mine, and as she threaded our fingers together, I swallowed hard.

"You're just trying to soften me up so that I don't kick your ass at cards later," she teased.

I exhaled sharply, trying not to show how she was affecting me.

"Yeah, you got me."

The next song started—a mid-tempo number that left little room for conversation. I led her easily; she was good at following my cues, and her eyes sparkled with laughter as I twirled her around the room. I liked seeing her happy, even if being so close to her was driving me insane with a mix of desire and jealousy.

Looking over at John, he still wasn't paying attention to anything except his conversation with Danny and Oisín, who'd joined in. This stunning woman was right there, waiting for him, *wanting* him, and he couldn't even look at her? Meanwhile, I hadn't stopped looking at her since the dance began.

Yet he'd be the one going home with her at the end of the night. Not me.

The song ended, and Isla must've noticed I was distracted, because she said, "You okay?"

I shook my head to clear it and looked down at her, forcing a small smile.

"Yeah, fine," I answered. "Just wondering what they're talking about over there."

Isla shrugged. "Think it has something to do with the PNCs. But I'd rather not talk about it. That debate earlier was plenty."

I nodded. "Fair enough. Want to dance again?"

"Yeah," she replied, giving me another heart-melting smile. "I do."

The new song was slow, so I swayed gently with her, and she stared up at me with a tenderness that felt dangerous. I wanted to kiss her, even with everyone—including her boyfriend—watching.

It was a bad idea. A disaster waiting to happen. So I did the only thing I could do.

I took my hand from hers and stopped turning us to the music.

"I'm a bit tired," I said, even though I wasn't. "Wanna play cards instead?"

She frowned at my hand, as if surprised to see it no longer in hers.

"Noah," she said in a very different tone—soft, intimate. She reached as if to touch my face, then seemed to think better of it and withdrew. "D'you think—?"

She didn't get to finish her thought. John had reappeared at her side, and she immediately put a smile on her face for him, though it looked strained.

"Sorry to interrupt," he said, shooting a glance at me before refocusing on Isla, "but we're heading out now. You still coming home with us?"

Isla nodded. "Just let me grab my bag."

She walked towards Kimmy, who still sat with her grandmother.

"Good to see you, man," John said, clapping me on the shoulder, and all I could manage was a nod before he followed her.

I watched her go with lead in my chest. Was I ever gonna be able to let her go? Stop carrying a torch that she clearly didn't want?

I tried dancing with some of the other girls after Isla left, and the answer became obvious: no, I would never be able to let her go, because even though they seemed interested enough in me, I could only nod politely to whatever they said. None of them held a candle to her, and I couldn't imagine in a thousand years feeling about them the way I did about her. More than that, I didn't *want* to. I'd loved Isla for so long that she was a part of me now, and I couldn't cut her out any more than I could cut off a limb.

And just like that, it was over, and I was heading back to my cabin alone again. My real-life desert island, only my desert island girl was nowhere in sight.

Chapter 3

Isla

The whole way back to Summerhurst, I wondered what I'd done to deserve what Kimmy had told me on that dance floor.

"Don't take this the wrong way," she'd said hesitantly. "I'm telling you this because I care about you, and I don't want to see you get hurt, okay?"

"Okay," I answered, baffled.

"What you said before, about you and John's wedding...have you talked to him about that before?"

I balked. "Uh...no. But I mean, we've been going out a while, so..."

Kimmy clucked her tongue sympathetically, which made me bristle a little.

"Isla, honey...I don't think John is in the same place you are."

I blinked at her. "What? Why?"

"Because I know him better than anyone," she said with a sigh. "He wants to be an outrider. That's why he's been doing all those drills on horseback that you saw the other day when you were over."

I frowned. Outriders were the team that patrolled the perimeter of the Valley on horseback, keeping us safe. Essentially soldiers, they were the best of the best when it came to combat and survival.

John had never even mentioned it to me.

"It's what Granddad did before he retired," Kimmy continued. "He's not in the headspace right now to commit to anyone...and the truth is, he may never be. He's not the type, much as Granny wishes otherwise."

"What are you telling me, then?" I asked, sounding more accusatory than I wanted. " That he doesn't want me?"

"No," Kimmy said quickly. "Not at all. He cares for you; I know he does. Just...just don't get your hopes too high, okay?"

My eyes burned. She was wrong. She had to be wrong. I'd known John my whole life, and I'd fantasized about dating him since I was fifteen. He was beloved by most of our community, and he was my brother's best friend. It was written in the stars or something, I was sure of it.

By the time we made it back to Summerhurst, I'd convinced myself that what Kimmy said was just her overreacting. I'd talk to John and we'd laugh about it. I hoped.

Kimmy and Aoife both said goodnight immediately and went upstairs to bed, while Oisín and John sat on the back porch talking. I had a glass of water in the kitchen before joining John on the porch swing.

"Don't stay up too late, son," Oisín said, nodding at John. "Strawberry picking tomorrow, and woe betide you if I make it out there and they're still there."

John rolled his eyes. "Don't worry, old man, I'll be out there."

"The cheek of this one, Isla," Oisín said to me, shaking his head. "If you know how to tame that tongue of his, you let me know, won't you?"

I laughed. "Can't promise much. Remember that Danny's my brother, sir."

Oisín grinned. "True."

He turned to John again and his expression suddenly turned serious. "Think about what I said, John."

John nodded, looking a little grave, before Oisín said goodnight and made his way into the house, leaving us sitting on the swing together. I pulled my legs up to my chest and turned to face John. He'd been quiet for most of the evening, unlike himself.

"What's got you brooding so much?" I said, raising an eyebrow.

He gave a small half-smile, staring out into the darkness beyond the porch.

"Just thinking about what a hard time we had finding PNCs today," he said with a sigh. "Every trip, we find less. Granddad was saying earlier that eventually, we're going to have to branch out into a much bigger search area. This far north, away from most cities, there are only so many places left to look."

"Yeah, I guess so," I said, not sure how to respond. "But we won't run out. The council will figure it out."

John shrugged. "Don't want to stake my future on that."

"It'll be fine," I answered, wanting to push past whatever mood he was in. "You want to go for a walk?"

He raised an eyebrow. "In the dark? Alone?"

"You scared?" I said, grinning.

He laughed. "No. But I figured you might be. You've never liked being outside at night much."

"I mean, would you, if Danny had once posed as a gang member and tackled you in the middle of the field after dark, in his idea of a 'fun prank'?"

John laughed again. "I guess not."

He still seemed reluctant, but after much pleading, he finally agreed. It was very warm for early October, and despite my fear of the darkness, I was enjoying it. I reached out for John's hand, which he let me take, though he didn't seem enthusiastic. He was still quiet while we walked, seeming like he was somewhere else. He'd been like this a lot lately with me, but I didn't understand why.

He'd never been much of a 'feelings' guy, but he was also rarely speechless. I watched him with concern, but his face didn't show anything. He was beautiful, really; all high cheekbones, soft brown eyes, and light skin that seemed permanently tanned. His long, dark hair was unusual in its style, and eye-catching. Tall and lean, but built solid with an obvious layer of well-developed muscle, I admired him, as I'd done most of my life. I wanted to make him forget anything that wasn't me.

We were near the edge of the woods when I stopped walking and tugged on John's hand. He turned to face me, and I kissed him. He kissed me back, gentle but still distracted. I pulled him in deeper, wanting to keep him here.

"I want you," I said softly when we broke apart. "Won't you take a minute from your brooding to sleep with your girlfriend, at least?"

He didn't laugh like I thought he would. He held my hands in his, glancing back in the direction of the house.

"No one's around," I said with a smile. "It's too dark for anyone to see anyway."

I kissed him again, and he returned it, a little more involved now. I backed up against a tree, pulling him with me and sighing. I felt over the planes of his body, and he sighed too. I knew when he stopped to run his lips down my neck that he'd surrendered at last, and I was glad.

I reached down to touch him. He groaned softly but didn't move. He was always gentle, something I appreciated but also found frustrating. He was never wild with the sort of passion I'd read about in my grandmother's decaying old stash of romance novels. He didn't want me like those men seemed to want their heroines...but I wanted him, wanted him to gasp and claw at me and call my name.

Kimmy's words came back to me. *He's not in the same place as you.* I tried to bat them away, but like an annoying fly, they stuck around, buzzing in my ear. Meanwhile, John kissed me with interest, but very little passion.

"John," I said, trying to keep the frustration out of my voice as I pulled back. "Don't you want me?"

He frowned. "What do you mean? Is this not okay?"

"It's not that," I said with a sigh. "I just...I want more. I want you so much that it hurts. Don't you ever feel that way?"

He hesitated, and a rush of impulsive emotion seized me.

"I think I'm falling for you," I said. "And I...I want you to make love to me. Like you mean it. Like you love me, too."

Dead silence. I couldn't see his face in the dark, so I waited, giving him time to answer. But the silence stretched on so long that it was obvious he wasn't going to. Tears pricked my eyes.

"You don't love me," I said, my voice breaking. It wasn't a question.

"I didn't say that," John replied defensively.

"You didn't have to."

He sighed heavily. "I'm sorry. Look, it's...it's not you, Isla."

"Really? 'It's not you, it's me'?" I said with a sarcastic laugh. "Is that really what you're going with?"

"No," he said miserably. "It really isn't you. You're a great girl. You're sweet, and fun, and..."

"And?" I demanded. "And not good enough for you?"

"No," he said again, agitated. "It has nothing to do with that. I don't know if I can feel that way. Not just about you. About anyone. I've been with other girls before and it's the same thing."

"So why would you lead me on?" I shot back.

"Not like I planned it that way," he said dryly. "I didn't know you felt like this till just now. For all I knew, we were just having fun together."

"But we've been together for...months," I said with difficulty. "I thought about us getting married. Having children. I thought...I figured you'd want that, too. Someday."

John sighed again. "If that's how you feel, then you deserve to be with someone who wants the same things you do. Who can love you the way you deserve."

My tears fell. "And that isn't you."

The suffocating silence was enough of an answer. A small sob escaped against my will. He hesitated for a moment, then gently cupped my cheek, wiping my tears with his thumb.

"I'm sorry," John murmured. "I didn't mean to hurt you. I care about you, Isla. I never wanted it to end like this."

The word *end* brought on a fresh wave of tears.

"So, this is over, then?" I whispered. "Just like that?"

"It has to be," he said, sounding regretful. "I won't break your heart like this again, because I can't give you what you need."

I felt twisted up with pain. Kimmy had tried to warn me. And like an idiot, I'd ignored her.

"I know that there's someone out there for you," John said, withdrawing his hand. "But I can't let you become even more invested in us, and then tell you that I don't love you, crushing your hopes and dreams."

He didn't understand that he'd already done that. I turned away.

"I have to go," I said, swiping at my tears and attempting a casual laugh that came out squeaky. "Thanks for the memories and all that. I know they meant something to me, even if they didn't to you."

"That's not—"

I ignored him and strode away in what I hoped was an outraged, dignified sort of way...until I stumbled on a rock I didn't see and nearly fell on my face. To John's credit, he didn't laugh, but his footfalls followed me. Apparently, dumping me mid-makeout sesh wasn't enough humiliation.

"Isla, wait!" John called, concerned. "It's dark. Let me at least walk you home."

"Not going home," I called back, finally finding my fury. "Just stay away from me, John Madigan. I'm a big girl. I'll be fine."

He stopped, framed by darkness, staring after me with regret and irritation. What *he* had to be irritated about, I didn't know, but I didn't stay to find out. I let the night swallow me up the way I wished the ground would, until the image of John faded away—no more significant than a shadow.

***

Thunder rumbled overhead and I was pelted with rain as I tried to find my way through the darkness, flashlight in hand. It gave me time to appreciate just how dumb I was, walking off into the night alone. If I'd been going home, it might've been less stupid; our homestead was relatively close to Summerhurst. But Noah's was farther, and so I had plenty of time to think.

The signs were there, I thought miserably. John never talked about the future. He never talked about how he felt about me or about any of the things I wanted—marriage, children, a home. Had I really known him at all? I'd never even known he wanted to be an outrider until Kimmy told me.

He was my brother's best friend and had been around me my whole life. I thought that meant I knew him, but as I looked over our relationship, I struggled to recall moments of real connection between us. We'd had fun together while horseback riding or hunting...and we'd had more than a little fun in the sack. John was kind, warm, and well-liked by almost everyone in the Valley. That made him seem perfect to me.

But when had he ever told me about his hopes and dreams? When had he told me about his fears, his insecurities, or the things he worried about? More importantly, when had I asked or cared about the answer? When he told me about what Oisín had said about the PNCs, I'd only wanted to push past that and get to the good part—the part where he made me feel beautiful and desirable, and where I got what I wanted from him.

Damn it, was I really that selfish?

The more I thought about it, the more it dawned on me that I'd been far more in love with the *idea* of John than the man himself. He was the hot, popular guy that every girl in our small community fawned over, and when he'd shown an interest in *me,* well, I'd forgotten much else besides his dashing good looks and taut, muscled body. Personality-wise, he was charming, but again, I realized I didn't know anything deeper than that. And here I was, thinking I was head over heels for him? I was such an idiot.

As rain clung to my skin and soaked my hair, I realized that the one person I *could* say that about—that I knew his hopes, dreams, fears, and doubts—was the same person who, at this moment, I was most anxious to see. Noah was a fixture in my life and had been since before I could talk. He was my one constant—my rock in the middle of an ocean of chaos. His presence calmed me, and being with him was...easy. I didn't have to try.

Eventually, my flashlight outlined the dark shape of Noah's small cabin, illuminating it with an eerie glow in the rain. Two years ago, on his eighteenth birthday, he'd moved out of the family's Old World house and, with the help of his father and my brother, built himself a small wood cabin on the Harding homestead. It was one room, with a little kitchenette, a living area with a fireplace, and a bed in the corner, a door to a tiny bathroom beside it.

I'd poked fun at the small space when he'd shown it to me, but in true Noah fashion, he'd simply shrugged and said it was enough for him, and besides, they'd built it so that he could easily add rooms. At least it was separate from the main farmhouse, so the entire Harding family wouldn't witness my shame.

I made it to the door, raised my hand to knock, then hesitated. I didn't think about what I'd do once I got there, except that...Noah was the one I went to when I had news, the person I shared the most with. And as stiff and serious as he could come across, I could make him laugh. He talked easily to me, even as he struggled to say more than a few words to others. Being with him was vital, necessary, and most of all, *easy.*

And our kiss...I'd refused to think about it while dating John, because it felt like a betrayal. But that one kiss with Noah was dearer to my heart than the entire relationship with John, and that should've told me something. When he kissed me, it felt like time stood still. But somehow, I'd locked all that away in a tight box inside me because of a childish daydream about a guy that, as it turned out, I barely even knew.

The curtains flicked in the window by the door, and a half-second later, I jumped as it suddenly opened. Noah appeared, dressed in loose linen pants and a sleeveless tank that I was pretty sure he threw on about thirty seconds before, a shotgun at his side. As usual, he took up most of the doorframe—he was at least twice my size. I took in the lines of his muscular frame, his arms and chest well-developed from a lifetime of farm work. He had the nicest grey eyes; they always showed the depth of feeling underneath his hard shell, if you looked hard enough. His brown beard definitely moved him into 'mountain man' territory...but as it happened, I was pretty into it.

I'd always known, on some level, that I was attracted to him, but I'd pushed those thoughts away because he was my best friend...and, well, I'd been dating someone else for too long.

The thought that he normally slept naked—something I'd known about him for years—suddenly made me flush for no good reason. His eyebrows rose as he took in my soaking wet, red-nosed appearance.

"What on God's green earth are you doing?" he said, his slight Southern twang coming out. "It's like ten o'clock and raining cats and dogs, and you're alone? You know better. Get in here."

He stepped aside and I followed him into the cabin, shutting the door behind me as he stashed his shotgun away. The main room was dark except for a single, spare light bulb hanging from the ceiling. Noah's cabin was sparsely furnished, but homey enough, with a large, wing-backed armchair by the fireplace, and a crocheted rug on the floor next to his bed—one I made for him when he first moved into the cabin. In fact, most of the sparse decor in his house were things I made—from the blanket folded at the foot of his bed to the cushion on his armchair with a cute pumpkin pattern on it. I hadn't wanted his place to feel empty or lonely for him, especially with how much he tended to isolate himself.

He needed a reminder that someone loved him.

Noah closed the door behind him and turned to look at me. His grey eyes reflected confusion and concern, but he waited for me to speak.

"I just wanted to talk," I said, but there was a tremor in my last word that I hated.

He frowned but didn't say anything. Clearly, I owed him a better explanation, but I didn't know if I could do it without crying, and I'd done enough of that tonight. Awful silence stretched out between us.

"What's wrong, kitten?" Noah finally asked, his voice achingly gentle, and hearing his nickname for me somehow broke me down all over again.

I buried my face in my hands and sobbed. Shame and humiliation came out at once, but I couldn't seem to stop it.

"Ah, hell," he murmured, clucking his tongue, and suddenly his arms were around me, pulling me against his big, warm body. I buried my face in his shoulder and wailed like a fucking baby. Everything I thought I wanted was gone. Worse, I didn't even know why I'd wanted it in the first place.

"John doesn't want me," I managed to blubber. "Doesn't love me. And I was so stupid, thinking he did, when I didn't even want to know him."

I told him the whole humiliating story.

"Isla, you aren't stupid," Noah said after I finished, and his voice, his arms around me, were so sweet and soothing. "You want what we all want: somebody to love. And he's crazy if he doesn't want a girl like you.

I shook my head against his shoulder. "Not crazy. All I cared about was that he was hot and popular. I loved the idea of him more than who he really was."

"He's charismatic," Noah replied, a hint of bitterness in his voice. "But you're sweet, and beautiful, and you've always deserved more than a roll in the hay. Which, hate to say it—he's a friend—but that's all John is ever gonna give you. He's a good guy, but I've never seen anyone really get close to him besides Kimmy."

Something in his tone made me step back, but he didn't let me go far. He held onto my forearms, keeping me close to his body. I dared to glance up at him. His trademark frown was still there, but underneath it was something else—an intensity, a storm of emotions he was holding back. He hesitated, gazing at me, before I saw in his eyes that he'd made a decision.

"Noah," I started, but didn't get to finish.

He leaned down and gently brushed his lips against mine, testing, feeling me out.

Sudden pleasure flooded my body, heating my skin underneath my cold, soaked clothes. His lips were warm and surprisingly soft against mine, which felt frozen from the rain. The kiss was undemanding, but there was definitely a question behind it. I answered with a little moan, pressing up against him and kissing him back.

A deep groan came from his chest. I opened my mouth, meeting his tongue with mine. He inhaled sharply, then pushed away from me.

"We should stop," Noah said gruffly, but his eyes were wild with need. There was so much hunger there. I wanted it to swallow me up.

A slow-burning heat started in my belly, egging me on.

"Why?" I asked, raising my eyebrows. A challenge.

He made a disgruntled noise. "Because you just cried in my arms about your ex. I shouldn't have...I mean, you're all confused right now. About what you want."

I shook my head slightly, then said in a low voice, "I know exactly what I want."

He tried to hide the small shudder that went through him, but I knew. I thought of our kiss a year ago—which I'd derailed with my stupid second-guessing—and wanted a different ending to that story.

"Tell me you want me to go," I said softly, reaching up to trace his bottom lip with my thumb. "Just say the words."

He flinched as though my touch had given him a shock. A muscle jerked in his jaw, clenched tight. His face was an emotionless mask like always, but I knew him. He needed this as much as I did—he just wasn't ready to admit it.

"Noah," I murmured, then rubbed my body against his. "Either kiss me, or—"

He grabbed my face in his hands almost violently. His tongue speared into my mouth with force, and I whimpered in surprise as his hand twisted in my wet hair. The heat of him was almost unbearable on this humid summer night, but the ache in my pussy was worse.

Noah pushed me hard against the cabin wall and pinned me. His mouth moved to my neck, kissing and sucking, and not gently—each one was edged with pain that he then soothed with his tongue. I felt drunk, grinding against him and making silly, desperate noises.

"Jesus," Noah breathed. "You don't know how long I wanted this."

"How long?" I asked.

"Years," he replied raggedly. "And since you've been with him, I've been losing my damn mind. Knowing he got to touch you like this. And feeling like you didn't even see me, when all I've been able to think about lately is having you."

His possessive tone should *not* have turned me on as much as it did. I should've been thinking about how I didn't need a rebound right now, and how this might ruin our friendship. I should've felt worse about kissing Noah right after John ended things. I should've given it time and not jumped right into bed with someone else...much less my best friend.

But sometimes a girl was just horny, and lonely, and heartbroken.

So I kissed him like I was dying. Like the sun was about to explode, destroying the Earth, and this was my last chance. I kissed him like I needed him to survive.

Noah groaned at my passion, and I steered him toward the big armchair in the middle of the living area. Stupid as it was when he was so much bigger, I pushed him. Solid and huge, he towered over me and didn't move an inch, but obviously took pity on me and sat down.

I straddled his lap and felt his cock brush against me through his loose-fitting pyjama pants. I ground hard against him, satisfied by the grunt that came from deep in his chest.

I kissed him again, longer this time, and feeling his cock harden under me was thrilling. But what was more was the way Noah kissed me back: not guarded, not holding back the way he usually did. He clawed at my wet tank top, and my nipples perked up in response.

He kissed me like he wanted me desperately. Like I was the only woman in the world. Like he needed me, and I mattered.

He frantically stripped away my shirt as we kissed. My breasts bounced free from my bra, and his mouth was instantly on them. I gasped at the way he sucked my nipple into his mouth. A thread of pleasure traveled straight to my pussy. His kisses and licks turned to small bites, leaving behind red marks that I loved seeing. I ground my clit against him as he kept going, feeling myself getting wetter by the second.

My need for him couldn't be ignored. I slid off his lap, between his knees, and grabbed hold of the waistband of his pants. Before he could react, I pulled them down, revealing his cock. I almost blushed at how big he was. I mean, he was a big guy, so I guessed I should've known, but still.

Alright, Noah. I see you and your massive dick.

I licked the underside of his cock, and he gasped.

"Isla—"

He drew in another breath as I closed my mouth around him. There was no way I could deep throat him, so I took as much of him as I could and worked him with my tongue. He leaned back in his chair with a groan.

"Isla," he murmured again, biting his lip. "You're the hottest little thing I ever saw."

The compliment pleased me, and I slid my mouth up and down his thick length. Then I sucked hard. He shuddered, groaned, then came all at once. His come hit the back of my throat, and I coughed a little, but managed to take it all. I loved knowing the secret taste of him.

Panting, Noah stroked my hair, looking at me with something like awe. It made me giggle.

"What?" he said with a rare smile.

I snorted. "You're just looking at me like you're...mesmerized, or something."

His smile faded, replaced by the affectionate look that he'd given me my whole life. The one that I'd never seen him give anyone else.

"I am," he said softly. "You're so perfect. Like always."

My heart did a little dip. I'd wanted this my whole life—to be desperately desired by someone. I didn't think that person would be Noah, if only because of my infatuation with John. I'd spent a lot of time pining after the wrong guy. But maybe this could be different. Maybe there was reason to hope.

Noah interrupted my thoughts by taking me by the hands and pulling me to my feet as he stood.

He bent and kissed me again, then growled, "Your turn."

I squealed as he hefted me up over his shoulder like a fucking haybale. He laughed, walked the short distance to his bed, and flopped me down onto it. I didn't have time to react, because he immediately peeled off my soaking pants and panties. He ditched his shirt and climbed on top of me.

His broad shoulders and big, muscled body were every girl's fantasy. I definitely didn't mind the view.

He gave more rough, hungry attention to my breasts. I arched and moaned. My clit throbbed with every touch until I couldn't take it. I pushed against him, and he let me roll him onto his back.

"I want to ride your tongue," I snarled, practically feral with need.

Without waiting for his answer, I straddled his face. To my delight, he pulled down hard on my hips, and my pussy was suddenly on his mouth. He gave me a long stroke from pussy to clit, and I gasped embarrassingly loudly.

The way Noah licked me was unpracticed, but whatever he lacked in experience, he made up for with enthusiasm. He swept through my folds over and over, eating me out with a hunger that made my toes curl, his beard lightly tickling my inner thighs. I rode his tongue shamelessly, burning with the need to break apart. My pussy fluttered, and I let out a sob as I came, hard and messy, as Noah grunted under me.

I threw myself onto the bed, panting. Noah joined me, wiping his soaked mouth on the back of his hand. It turned me on to see traces of my come on his beard, around his lips. He kissed me, and things quickly heated up again. He rolled on top of me, and soon, I felt his cock harden again between us.

"I want..." Noah hesitated. "I want to take you. Can I?"

"Yeah," I answered breathlessly. "It's one of my safe days."

He kissed me, gentle this time. "Good. I'll pull out."

His hand went between my legs, gathering my wetness on his fingers before stroking his cock. Making himself slick with *me*. My pussy clenched.

I lay back, and Noah eased himself inside me. I whimpered a little at the size of him, stretched and a bit uncomfortable. He was patient and sweet, holding still and kissing me while he waited for me to adjust.

Finally, I relaxed, and he started to fuck me. Slow and deep at first, then faster once I was used to the feel of him. He grunted with each thrust, the corded muscles in his arms standing out as he held himself above me.

I met his eyes. He looked at me like I was the single most desirable thing in the world. Like I was oxygen, or food to a starving man. I could get used to being looked at like that.

"You're so beautiful, kitten," he panted. "Just like I always imagined."

He suddenly pulled out and flipped me over onto my front. I moved onto my hands and knees as he positioned himself behind me. He teased me briefly with the head of his cock at the entrance to my pussy.

I made an impatient sound, and he smiled. Then he pushed back into me. I moaned and curled my fingers around the sheets as he started thrusting again.

"You imagined fucking me like this?" I gasped out.

"A hundred times," Noah murmured. "Fucked my fist to thoughts of your mouth on me, your hot pussy around me, more times than I can count."

He held me steady, his hand on my lower back, while he fucked me harder, faster. The angle was better for me in this position. I rubbed my clit clumsily, and an orgasm built at my centre. Another moment and it broke, and I let out a breathless cry as I came again, covering Noah's cock.

Noah gave a satisfied grunt and kept going until he pulled out with a ragged gasp. He gave himself a couple rough pumps with his hand, then groaned deeply as he came on my lower back. He collapsed over me, his chest to my back, and turned my head to kiss me.

I kissed him back with my whole heart. It felt natural. Like something we should've been doing all along.

"Made a mess between us," he said after a moment, amused. "Gimme a sec."

He got up to fetch a towel from his bathroom, then wiped his semen from his front and my back. Then he got into bed with me, scooping me up in his arms and holding me against his big, warm body.

It was kind of like lying with a giant teddy bear. I didn't hate it.

It'd been a long, confusing night. I was sure I'd have some questions to answer in the morning, but I didn't care. All I wanted now was to snuggle against Noah and know that right now, everything was okay.

"That was amazing," I said, leaning my head against his chest.

He pressed his lips against my head but didn't say anything at first. Finally, he said, "Was everything I ever wanted."

Satisfied, I sighed, and fell asleep.

Chapter 4

Isla

The sun was up by the time I woke the next morning. Farm life meant that I was usually up at dawn, but it was later than usual. I groaned and rubbed my eyes, then reached for Noah, but the bed was empty. He'd probably gotten up to do his morning chores. Which I should also be doing, and Danny would be mad at me getting home so late in the day, but to be fair, I'd told him that I'd be staying overnight...okay, at John's, but same difference.

The breakup was the furthest thing from my mind that morning. I should've been stunned by that, but I wasn't. The guy I'd been crushing on for years dumped me, and somehow...I didn't really care? Who was I?

I stretched and lay back on the pillows, remembering the night before. Noah woke me during the night and took me again with the same hungry, urgent need as before. After we finished, he held me again, kissed me, told me how beautiful I was.

It was different from the awkward, hesitant kiss he'd given me last year. He hadn't held back. He'd been open with his desire, vulnerable in a way I didn't know Noah was capable of.

And I felt so...whole. Complete. Like this had been a missing piece of the puzzle that I didn't realize I didn't have until I got it.

I'd been chasing a dream of falling in love that didn't match reality. I thought falling in love was something that just sort of happened, like magic. I thought falling in love was like a recipe: mix one hot, popular guy with one eager girl, bake for a year, and boom, fairytale romance.

But it wasn't that. It was in Noah's sweet childhood nickname for me. The way he let me have the last bite of pie. All the little moments of easy chatter and laughter throughout our lives. All the memories and big, important things he'd been there for. All the times he'd cheered me up and cheered me on.

I loved him. And the thought of being with him didn't make me anxious; it made me happy. It wouldn't be something new and scary, nor would it be like trying to force a square peg into a round hole. It'd be a natural extension of what we already were to each other.

I got up out of bed and looked for my clothes. I spotted them through the window, flapping lightly in the breeze on the clothesline. Noah must've hung them to dry when he got up. A small gesture, but he'd always been thoughtful like that.

Or at least...he had been for me.

It was probably fine to go outside naked to get them—nobody was around—but on the off-chance that Noah's parents or siblings happened to be nearby, I didn't want to risk showing them my ass. Instead, I walked to the kitchen area to look for something to eat.

By the time Noah got back, I had eggs sizzling in a cast iron pan, along with Noah's homemade bread and danishes. His baking skills were one of the many things you wouldn't assume just by looking at him. Most people wouldn't think that those big hands could create delicate pastries with such care, or that his stoic demeanour would allow him to be gentle or sweet. Any softness he had came out in little ways—ways he could easily hide from everyone. Everyone but me.

Noah gave me a once-over as he walked through the door. He tried to hide it, but his eyes lingered a second too long on my naked body. As usual, he didn't smile at me. But I didn't take that as a bad sign; that was just how he was.

"Hey," I said with a shy smile, crossing my arms over my bare breasts. "You want something to eat?"

He ignored the question and held out my clothes. "Here. They're dry. You should get dressed."

I raised an eyebrow but took them from him. I watched him carefully as I got dressed, but he didn't look at me. He just walked to his small dining table and sat down, staring at the polished wood. Odd, but maybe he wasn't in a talkative mood.

I finished cooking and set the plates on the table before sitting across from him to eat. He didn't say anything as we ate except a murmured thank-you. After we finished, I loaded the dishes into the sink and started the water.

"I'll do it," Noah said, neatly inserting himself between me and the sink. "You should head home. It's late enough that your folks'll be wondering."

I frowned. His tone was flat and detached.

"What's wrong?" I asked. My stomach felt suddenly queasy.

"Nothing," he answered, a little too quickly. "Just know your brother's gonna be looking for you soon. Didn't think you'd want him to find you here."

"Why wouldn't I want that?" I said, folding my arms. "Noah. Look at me."

He didn't. Instead, he picked up a brush and scrubbed the dishes like they'd personally offended him. My impatience boiled over.

"What's gotten into you? Why are you acting like last night didn't happen?"

"I'm not," he replied, setting a clean dish on the rack. "It was a great night, kitten. I know it's what you needed after the breakup."

My eyebrows shot up as far as they could go. "So that's what it was? Pity sex?"

He still wouldn't look at me. "No. But I know it didn't mean anything."

I felt as though he'd punched me in the gut.

"It didn't?" I said softly, and I hated that I heard the hurt in my voice.

Noah sighed. "You really gonna do this with me, Isla? We both know that as soon as you lick your wounds, you'll be trying to get John's attention again. He's what you really want. What you've always wanted."

"Oh, and you know what I want?" I shot back.

"Yeah, I do," he said, and for the first time, there was something like anger in his voice. He threw down the scrubbing brush, and it splashed in the sink. "You've been my best friend since I was in diapers. And that's how I know that this was just a rebound for you. Something you needed for comfort. It was amazing for one night, but...that's it."

My heart broke for the second time in two days. Only this felt worse. My best friend in the whole world was rejecting me. He hadn't felt the completeness that I did after we'd had sex. He was just comforting me because that's what he thought I needed.

"I didn't do it because I wanted comfort," I said, my throat suddenly dry. "I...I wanted *you.*"

"That's what I thought after our first kiss," Noah replied, detached again. "But then you got with him, not me. And this time, you only wanted me because you couldn't have him anymore."

I swallowed hard. The problem was that he wasn't entirely wrong. But being with him the night before—the way he'd touched me, and held me, and made love to me—had changed everything in my eyes. I saw things clearly now, the way I would've if I'd bothered to look before...if I hadn't been trying to force the happy ending I thought I wanted.

I'd been selfish and stupid. And now, I was reaping what I'd sown.

"I'm not gonna be your second choice," he continued. "Your fallback guy. I can't."

"That's not what you are to me," I whispered. "How could you think that?"

"How could I not?" he countered, then finally looked at me. I wasn't prepared for how much pain there was in his deep brown eyes. "You can say now that you feel different, but I've known you too long. I just can't believe you, kitten. I wish I could."

The childhood nickname hit like a blow.

"Don't call me that," I spat, my own eyes aching from holding back tears.

Noah went back to washing dishes as though I hadn't said anything.

He was wrong about how I felt, but I couldn't blame him. I couldn't really argue with him, either, because his judgment of me was justified. I'd made a real mess of things and blew my chance with the one guy I could see a realistic future with. After a solid minute of dish-washing, it was obvious that he was done talking to me.

"Alright," I said brokenly. "I'll just...I'm gonna go home."

He nodded, his face unreadable, but his eyes said everything.

"I think that'd be best."

Who knew those simple words held the power to break my heart all over again?

***

"You moping in here again?"

I rolled my eyes, even though I *was* moping. Very much so. Still, Danny annoyed me on his best day, so with how shitty the last week had been, he was completely unbearable now. He'd made so many jokes about the breakup, and I'd been so miserable that I'd just started coming up to my room after my work on the farm was done for the day.

I kept myself busy on a healthy regime of staring longingly out the window, pacing the room, and crocheting a stuffed duck. Because it wasn't something we needed, I'd used the leftover bits of yarn, which meant it was green, red, and pink, and absolutely fucking hideous. Noah would've said it was ugly as a sunburnt sow in heat.

"I'm trying to *read* here," I said, even though I wasn't. Sure, I had a book open on the bed in front of me, but I hadn't read a single word. The duck I was working on sat in my lap, but I'd barely made any progress on it today.

Danny huffed. "A likely story, especially because you haven't read a book since you were twelve."

"What do you want?"

Kitty mewed and pawed at my hair from her spot on my bed. After a week of hiding in my room with her, even she thought I was sort of pathetic.

I rolled over on the bed to face the door. "If you're just here to bug me, you're wasting your time. I've decided to live the rest of my life as a recluse."

"Think you need more than just the one cat to qualify for that," Danny replied, groaning as he lowered himself into the too-short chair by my cluttered writing desk. "When was the last time you actually wrote anything at this desk, sis? It looks like a dumping ground."

It *was,* but all I said was, "shut up, Danny," and made a stitch in my ugly-as-sin stuffed duck. His eye was pink and a little lopsided, making him look demented.

He paused, then cleared his throat. "Look, I know I'm bad at this shit, but I really *am* sorry that John broke up with you. If it helps, he feels terrible about it, especially knowing how hard you're taking it."

Yeah, so I hadn't told anybody about Noah. Everybody around here thought I was broken up about John, when the truth was, I'd barely given him any thought since the night we split up. I couldn't stomach telling anyone what'd really happened, though. It was too humiliating.

I'd tried going to Noah's every day this week, but he was always either gone or wouldn't answer the door. I even went up to the main farmhouse at Brookside and hounded his poor mom about him, who played it cool and told me she didn't know what he was up to. But she knew how close Noah and me were, and that we hadn't gone a week without seeing each other...maybe ever.

"It's fine," I said, hating that my voice wobbled. "I'm fine."

"Yeah, because you always sob alone in your room when you're fine," Danny observed, and I laughed as a tear spilled over.

He sat on the edge of the bed next to me and rubbed my back, the way he sometimes did when we were kids and I was sad about far smaller things. I swiped at my tears, but it was useless.

"It's okay," Danny said, gentler than I knew my brother was capable of. "You can cry. I'm not gonna burst into flames. I swear."

I gave another watery laugh, and then the dam broke. I sobbed helplessly into my pillow while my big brother rubbed my back in silence. When I'd finally cried myself out some time later, he spoke again.

"I know you're going through something right now," he said. "But all the more reason you shouldn't be holed up here by yourself all the time. Come downstairs. Kimmy's visiting—without John, I promise. He's busy with maintenance work at Summerhurst anyway."

I hesitated, but then nodded. He was probably right. Sitting up here didn't seem to be making things any better. And who knows? Maybe Noah just needed time. Maybe he'd come around.

I followed Danny to the living room, where my younger sister Jenna was sitting with Kimmy. Both of them were sitting on the sofa, giggling about something or other. My grandparents had probably already gone to bed.

"Hey," Kimmy said happily to me. "Good to see you coming out of that room. From what your sister tells me, you've been hanging out by yourself a lot lately."

"I guess," I said with a shrug.

"She's so mopey all the time now," Jenna said with an incredibly irritating little-sister eyeroll. "Boohoo, my way-hotter-than-me boyfriend dumped me."

I opened my mouth to say something rude, but Danny surprised me by interrupting.

"Cool it, Jen," he said, a warning in his voice. "Be nice."

Jenna huffed but shut up, thankfully. I gave Danny a grateful look as I sat in the empty armchair opposite the sofa.

"You should be getting to bed anyway," he said to our sister, who sighed dramatically. "Got school in the morning."

"I'm fifteen! Don't need a bedtime anymore."

"The way you cover your face with the pillow every morning when I wake you tells me differently," Danny replied. "Come on. Go."

With a grumble, she headed upstairs, and Danny followed after a quick goodnight. I appreciated him giving me some one-on-one time with Kimmy. My little mope session meant I hadn't seen her since the last dance.

"So, you're still taking it hard about John, huh?" she said sympathetically. "I get it, it sucks. But I hope you know that he never wanted to hurt—"

"I don't care about John," I burst out, sounding snappier than I meant to. I was just so tired of holding everything in.

Kimmy raised an eyebrow. "I know you're hurting right now, but—"

"I am," I said miserably, burying my face in my hands. "But not about John. I mean, yeah, him dumping me sucked, I guess, but..."

"What's wrong, then?"

I glanced up at Kimmy. Her big brown eyes were looking at me with concern. She had such a kind face; it was hard not to tell her stuff. I also didn't want to keep it to myself anymore. I needed a shoulder to cry on, and since it couldn't be Noah's, it might as well be Kimmy, who'd been like the big sister I'd never had for most of my life.

"Noah," I managed to get out, and my throat tightened. "I really fucked things up."

She sighed. "This about how he's desperately in love with you?"

I snorted. "I wish, especially considering he won't even speak to me."

Kimmy leaned back on the sofa, undoubtedly preparing herself to be there a while.

"Tell me all about it, then."

***

A couple weeks passed, and still nothing from Noah. I'd kept going to his place for a while, trying to catch him off-guard, but it never happened. Whatever was going on...it seemed he truly was done with me. After fifteen years of friendship. I couldn't think about it too long or I'd start crying again, and I was sick of that.

I tried to keep myself busy by visiting Kimmy at Summerhurst. She'd listened to me cry and throw myself a pity party that night she came over, and then expertly directed me towards other things: going on horseback rides together, helping Aoife with organizing the clinic, and of course, scavving. Since Noah kept trading scav shifts so that he wouldn't have to go with me, she took on scav duties again to go with me.

I hadn't seen John much since the breakup, even though I was visiting Summerhurst more often. I got the sense that he was avoiding me on purpose. When I asked Kimmy about it, she said he was trying to give me space. Well, space was just about the last thing I wanted, since I was a lonely moping mess lately, so I decided to clear the air.

I tracked him down to the workshop at Summerhurst, where he was apparently working on their old pickup truck. Not everyone in the Valley had old world electric vehicles—even aside from the priceless PNCs they needed, they were hard to find parts for, and getting them made by our local machinist was expensive—but they made life easier for those who had them.

The workshop was a large building with half-finished projects scattered around. The garage door was open, and John was bent over the truck's engine, fiddling with something or other and mumbling what sounded a lot like curses under his breath.

"Hey," I said awkwardly, standing in the doorway.

John started, then turned to look at me, wiping his hands on a rag he'd tucked into his belt.

"Hi," he replied, sounding slightly anxious. "Kimmy told me you were coming around today. Can I, uh...help you with something?"

"Yeah. Can we talk?"

He blinked twice. "Sure. Didn't think you'd want to talk to me."

I sat down on an overturned crate by the workbench.

"I know," I said. "But I wanted you to know I'm not mad at you anymore."

"Oh," he replied, leaning back against the truck, his arms folded. "Okay. That's good."

I laughed. "And this isn't me trying to get back together with you."

"Okay. So, what *do* you want?"

I sighed. "I don't know, I guess...I want us to be friends again, one day? I don't want it to be awkward between us forever. Besides that, I don't want to have to avoid you when I'm visiting. It's uncomfortable for Kimmy, and for all of us."

He nodded. "Sounds reasonable to me."

"But there's a catch."

John frowned. "A catch?"

"Yeah," I said. "I may not be mad at you, but you still dumped me. So, I curse you, John Madigan."

"What?" John said with a laugh.

I allowed myself a giggle too. "You said you haven't loved anyone before, and that you don't think you ever will. So, I curse you to find the love of your life, someone you can't be without, and then to know what it means to need another person so much that it steals your breath away. So much that it physically hurts to lose them."

My chest tightened unexpectedly. *That's how I feel about you, Noah. If you'd bother to listen to me.*

John raised his eyebrows. "That's quite the curse. I'll have to be on my guard."

I nodded. "And my curses have a bad habit of coming true."

He laughed again. "I'll keep that in mind."

I turned to go, but he said, "I know you love him, Isla. That's why I had to let you go."

I stopped dead in my tracks and turned, eyebrows raised.

"Did Kimmy—?"

"No," he answered, shaking his head. "I suspected it for a while, and then after you ran off that night we split up, I followed you. I just wanted to see you home safe, but...I saw you go to his place, which confirmed things."

My cheeks flooded with heat. "I'm sorry. I promise nothing happened while we were—"

He held up a hand. "It's fine. Really. Can't say it didn't hurt my ego, but...I've known you both forever, and you two make a lot of sense. More than you and I ever did, honestly."

A small smile formed on my lips. “You’re a lot more gracious than I deserve.”

He shrugged. “I told you the truth that night: we want different things. Breaking up was inevitable, even without you and Noah.”

I nodded. “I know that now.”

“Glad to hear it.”

We chatted easily after that, until Kimmy came looking for us and we all headed in together for dinner. It felt good to have my friends back, even as my heart still ached for the one friend I missed more than any of them.

Chapter 5

Isla

The following week, I had more scavenging duties, which was only interesting because I'd been assigned with Noah again...and unlike previous weeks, he hadn't managed to trade shifts with anyone. Kimmy was on nursing duty at the clinic, and nobody else had been able or willing.

It'd be the first time that I'd seen him in weeks. Part of me was terrified to be stuck with him when he'd barely said two words to me since we'd slept together, but another part of me was just mad. He'd never frozen me out like this before, and it didn't seem like he was going to stop anytime soon. After so many years of friendship, he wouldn't even consider actually *listening* to me. Prick.

So, when I walked through the doors of the Lodge, I wasn't sure what to expect. Would Noah be silent and unreachable? Or would he have changed his mind and be willing to talk?

I don't care, I thought, irritated. *I'm giving him a piece of my mind.*

What I didn't expect was that the anteroom, where we usually met with scav partners, would be empty. It wasn't like Noah to be late, but then again, he could be dragging his feet because he didn't want to talk to me. I rolled my eyes, impatient. He couldn't keep expecting me to just wait around for him to decide that feelings weren't too difficult for him.

Ten minutes passed, then twenty. I was starting to get uneasy. Where was he? Noah always showed up, no matter how reluctantly. Even when he grumbled about it, he was always there when I asked him to be, or when I needed him most. What could've happened to him?

Finally, I entered the main building, heading for the door to our medical clinic at the back. Whoever was on duty there may have seen or heard him if he'd been here. The clinic door was open, so I walked in.

We called it a clinic, but it was really just a room with an exam table, some carefully salvaged medical equipment from the Old World, and a few shelves of medicine, mostly made by one of the medical team. There was a small, closet-sized room in the back with a cot for critically injured people, but thankfully it wasn't used often.

As expected, Kimmy was there, chewing her lip and frowning slightly in concentration as she studied a medical chart. Her black hair was in its usual ponytail, and when her fringe fell into her eyes, she brushed it aside impatiently.

"Hey, Kim," I said, and she started.

"Sorry," she replied, setting down the chart. "Just in my own little world there. Isla. What do you need? Are you not feeling well?"

My stomach was in knots, but it had nothing to do with illness.

"Fine, thanks," I said uneasily. "Have you seen Noah around here today?"

A pit of dread opened up in my belly when she shook her head.

"Sorry, I haven't seen him. It's been pretty quiet around here, so I'd probably have noticed if he'd been in."

"He was supposed to meet me here for a scav mission. It's not like him to no-show. I'm...a little worried."

She nodded slowly. "Well, my shift is over in a few minutes. Maya's coming to relieve me, so if you can wait, I'll come with you to look for him."

"Thanks," I replied, relieved.

Maya arrived five minutes later, and after a brief conversation, Kimmy followed me out of the Lodge.

"John's picking me up," she said. "He can give us a ride to Noah's if you want."

I nodded. Much as it was probably weird to accept favours from my ex, I knew John would help us. It was how he was. And riding in his truck would be a lot faster than walking home to get my horse.

Sure enough, the black pickup came around the corner and up the dirt road toward us. John stopped in front of the Lodge, and we climbed in.

"Hey," he said with a small smile. "Didn't realize I was the designated driver today."

"Sorry," I said, but he waved it away. "I wouldn't ask, but..."

Kimmy explained Noah's absence, and John agreed to stop by Brookside to look for him. The ride to the homestead was quiet, and I kept trying to tell myself that he probably just forgot about me. That he'd be in his cabin and would scowl at me when I burst in, worried for nothing. I almost believed it.

But a bigger part of me knew something was wrong. Noah had never stood me up before. If he wasn't there, it was for a reason.

Sure enough, nobody answered my knock on the cabin door, and it was locked. I called for him, saying I only wanted to know he was safe, but again, silence. Frustrated, I marched back to the truck where John and Kimmy waited.

We decided to ask after him at the main farmhouse. Mrs. Harding, who was probably sick of me being on her doorstep, told me sympathetically that she hadn't seen him that day at all, then gently suggested that he might not want to talk to me. I didn't care. As soon as I knew that idiot was safe, I was going to skin him alive.

"Nothing?" Kimmy said, a note of worry in her voice now as I returned to the truck. "Anywhere else he could be?"

"No," I replied, feeling helpless. "I...it just doesn't feel right to me."

"Do you think he went without you?" John asked thoughtfully.

"Why would he do that?" I said, my voice almost a snarl, but immediately, the idea took root.

John shrugged. "I dunno, the girl I'm insanely in love with starts hanging out with her ex again, and maybe I'm pissed off about it and just don't want to see her. I mean, I don't know him as well as you do, but that sounds like something he'd do. The guy avoids shit."

"He's not in love with me," I objected. "If he was, he wouldn't have ignored me for weeks."

Kimmy chuckled. "Or that's why he's been ignoring you."

I hummed impatiently. "But why would he think we've been hanging out?"

"You've been at Summerhurst a lot lately," Kimmy said. "Not like he knows that it's mostly been to see me."

I sighed, frustrated. "But how would he even know? Not like he's let me tell him anything these past few weeks."

John snorted. "Like that matters? You know that gossip is like fucking air to the people in this community. Stuff gets around fast, and while I love my grandparents, they couldn't keep a secret to save their damn lives."

He's right, I admitted grudgingly. *So, Noah just takes off without even telling me?*

"He could be in trouble," I said, thinking out loud. "There's a reason we only scav in pairs. That's like, lesson one of scavving. Idiot."

There was a brief pause, where I silently fumed at Noah for putting me in this position, and wondered what the hell I was supposed to do about it.

"Guess we'd better go after him, then," John said casually, starting the truck again. "And make it fast. We're burning daylight, and I am not missing Granny's casserole night just because Noah's sulking."

"Psh, you know she'll save you a massive piece regardless," Kimmy said, rolling her eyes. "Can't let Grammy's special boy go hungry."

They bickered affectionately back and forth as we drove towards Summerhurst to drop off the truck, and all I could feel was gratitude for my friends and this tight knit community we were lucky enough to be part of. After the apocalypse, when everyone else had so much less than we did, it was nothing to take for granted.

***

We decided to go after Noah on horseback to save time. John and Kimmy retrieved their horses from Summerhurst, and then took me back home to get mine. I saddled up my horse, Blaze, trying to ignore my rotten mood. I couldn't believe that after weeks of silence, Noah was forcing *me* to chase after *him*. A part of me hoped he'd twist an ankle out there and have to spend a night outside—teach him a lesson.

But most of me was terrified of the small things that could go wrong out in the wilderness that would make it impossible to get home. Even minor injury could be a death sentence. I couldn't leave him out there alone.

I added a few extra arrows to my quiver before slinging it over my shoulder and mounting Blaze.

"You good?" Kimmy asked from her own mount. She and John had brought rifles, of course. They were some of the best shots I'd ever seen.

I nodded. Thank God my brother and sister were busy today, and I hadn't had to face their questions. Or, in the case of Danny, his terrible attempts to make light of things.

John clicked his tongue and his horse, Ghost, started walking. I'd always admired Ghost; she was silvery white, with deep, soulful black eyes and pretty grey markings on her snout. She'd been my brother's favourite when we were raising her. Kimmy did the same with her horse, Bella—a brown mare with a sweet, easygoing disposition, not unlike Kimmy herself.

The scav mission site was an old, abandoned hunting lodge. We rode hard to reach it within an hour. An enormous log cabin appeared on the horizon, its wooden construction worn and water-damaged, its face almost totally hidden by creeping ivy. A rusting metal fence surrounded it, dotted with huge holes that made it useless. A lonely dirt road snaked out in the direction of the old highway, but we were pretty far out. It was why this place had stayed relatively intact: it was in the middle of nowhere, hidden by dense forest, far from the gang-infested ruins of the few cities and towns that dotted the northern Ontario landscape.

Other members of the Valley's scav team had been here once before. I remembered them noting that there was a large gun safe in the basement, but at the time, they'd lacked the tools to open it.

We found a gap in the fence large enough for our horses to pass through and began our search.

"Noah?" I called, unable to keep the fear out of my voice. "Noah!"

Nothing. I wandered up to the door of the lodge, and just when I was about to turn the handle, it opened. Standing in the doorway, tall and intimidating as usual, was Noah.

He looked a bit more haggard than the last time I'd looked at him properly. There were shadows under his eyes, like he hadn't been sleeping. Despite my anger toward him, I was struck with sudden concern. His expression was hard and unyielding, and he gave me a cold look.

"What are you doing here?" he hissed at me, and I bristled.

"Saving your dumb ass," I retorted, hands on my hips. "What do you think you're playing at, hmm? Going out here alone? Least you could've done would be to tell me, but no, of course Noah has to go off on his own to prove he doesn't need anyone, as usual."

To prove he doesn't need me, I almost said, but I stopped myself just in time. Even though the thought made me miserable.

"Keep your voice down," he said, glaring at me. "I didn't need you to come after me. I can take care of myself."

I threw up my hands in frustration.

"So next time, I can leave you to the buzzards, huh? Good to know. I actually was worried about you, jerk, but I guess that doesn't mean anything to you anymore, does it?"

Silence. Just like always, he had nothing to say when confronted with the possibility of having feelings. Stubborn ass.

Distantly, I heard John call Kimmy over to wherever he was, his voice tinged with concern. Noah exhaled harshly, and my skin prickled with sudden awareness. Something was here with us.

The loud bang of a rifle shot shattered the air, and then the heavy sound of horse hooves hitting the ground, breaking into a gallop. I barely had time to gasp before Kimmy called out, "Maneaters!"

An inhuman shriek split the air—the way the maneaters called to one another, to draw more of them. Clearly, that was too much for Blaze, who reared wildly, snapping his reins. He bolted in the opposite direction towards the woods.

I automatically moved to follow him, but Noah grabbed my arm just as Kimmy called to John that more were coming.

"Find him later," he growled at me. "Get inside. We need higher ground."

Blaze's black tail disappeared into the trees.

"Damn it," I spat as Noah dragged me toward the door of the hunting lodge.

Noah pushed me through the doorway, then slammed the heavy wooden door shut behind him. I grabbed the nearest piece of furniture—an old wooden chair—and shoved it under the door handle. I didn't know if it'd hold, given the mouldering wood, but it was better than nothing.

"Upstairs," Noah barked, his shotgun in his hands now.

We raced up creaky, sagging wooden steps to the second floor. The only vantage points were the tiny windows in the front and back bedrooms. I took one and Noah covered the other. Outside was now a mess of bloodied corpses and enraged maneaters running in all directions. Most of them carried crude clubs and spears, shaking them violently as they continued their horrible shrieks, trying to call more of their tribe.

My breath caught at the sheer number of them. I'd never seen so many in one place before. There were dozens. I worried they'd swarm the building if we couldn't take them out quickly enough.

Kimmy was still on horseback, circling the swarm at the edge of the woods, firing off rifle rounds as she went. She mowed down a few of them, but eventually had to speed up to dodge the blows aimed at her horse. Several maneaters moved to cut her off and unseat her.

I slid my bow off my shoulder and aimed through the window, but the space was so tight that it was hard to get a clear shot. I managed to fire off an arrow, taking down one of the men trying to box her in, but more joined in. The vantage point was bad enough that I worried about hitting Kimmy or Bella by accident if I tried again.

"John!" Kimmy called frantically, but wherever he was, he wasn't close enough to help.

Noah barreled into the room with his rifle. He made it to the other window in the room and put in a few shots, keeping the maneaters around Kimmy at bay...for now.

"Go up!" he ordered. "There's a ladder up to the attic in the hall. I'll follow."

Thank God. I raced out into the second-floor hallway. At the end of the hall, a rusty ladder was bolted to the wall. I scrambled into the attic, coughing at the clouds of dust that rose up. It was full of mouldy old furniture—probably once a storage room. The windows up here were still small, but they were taller, and overlooked a roof ledge. The glass was long gone, and the floor was covered in bird shit. Lovely.

Perfect. I ran to the empty windowpane and squeezed through onto the ledge. From here, I had a clear view of the chaos at the treeline, where Kimmy was still trying to cut a path through the mass of bodies.

I took care to calculate each shot as I fired arrows into the crowd. Noah kept shooting from the lower level. Kimmy called again for John, and I could tell she was starting to panic. *Where the hell are you, John?* I thought desperately.

I barely finished the thought when John rounded the corner, urging Ghost forward at a rapid pace, his rifle in his arms. A group of maneaters chased after them, screaming and waving clubs and spears. He made a sharp turn to circle back around them, then fired off three shots. Three of the grimy men fell, but there were four still following him.

He charged into the maneaters surrounding Kimmy, scattering the group and trampling one of them. One didn't make it and was trampled. His agonized screams and the gruesome crunch of bones made me flinch. John kept firing as he went, carving a path for Kimmy. She followed him, urging Bella into a gallop.

Together, they circled the remaining cannibals in the same way they'd round up cattle. It forced the maneaters into a clustered mass in the centre. Round and round the two of them went in opposite directions, firing more shots and thinning them out, one by one.

Just as I was taking aim again, Noah's brown hair popped up above the attic hatch. I turned and waved him over to my prime shooting spot. He frowned at the sight of me on the roof but followed. His muscular frame barely fit through the window.

Together, we fired at the mob, and after a minute or two, the maneaters were in a death spiral. Most of them were down—either dead or groaning in pain. The last few standing were thrashing, trying to move through the mass of bodies to escape, but John and Kimmy had tightened the noose. Their circles got smaller and smaller, squeezing them into submission.

Within a couple minutes, the bloody horde lay dead or dying, and John and Kimmy had slowed to a trot. We had won.

I turned to give Noah a relieved smile when something hit me. By instinct, I touched my upper back. It felt wet and sticky, and when I looked at my fingers, they were deep red. Confused, I stared for what felt like a long time, but must've been less than a second.

There was another shriek from the maneaters. Two grubby men, separate from the rest, stood at the tree-line. John was already aiming at them, and in seconds, they were both on the ground, bleeding out.

One of them dropped a bow as he fell. *Oh.*

"Noah," I said, dizzy. "I feel weird."

My knees gave out, and I nearly toppled off the roof. Noah sprang forward and grabbed the strap of my backpack. He pulled me close enough to get an arm around me and keep me upright.

"Shit," he whispered, staring at the crude arrow lodged in my shoulder.

He dragged me back through the window, super-naturally fast, and lowered me face-first to the bird shit-covered floor. His big hands were achingly gentle. I coughed at the dust bunnies I was practically kissing. I didn't feel pain, even though I should've.

Noah stood frozen for a half-second, staring at me. Then he ran to the window.

"KIMMY!"

I'd never heard Noah sound like that.

His ragged scream carried a raw note that sounded like his world was ending.

You're dying, I thought idly. Weird that I wasn't more upset about it. I was too dizzy, and my shirt was wet and gritty, clinging to my skin unpleasantly.

Noah dropped to his knees next to me. He muttered frantically to himself as he rummaged through his pack for his first aid kit.

He tried to get the supplies out but dropped them; his hands were shaking too much. He examined the wound and paled.

"It's bad, isn't it?" I croaked. "I—"

"Shh," he soothed, pushing my hair out of my face. "You're okay, kitten. You're alright."

I didn't know if he was trying to reassure me or himself; his voice shook. He clumsily ripped off a strip of gauze and pressed it on my back, around the arrow. Pain suddenly stabbed me, so ferociously that I couldn't breathe. I could hear a thin, wheezing whimper. Just as I realized the sound was coming from me, Noah called out for Kimmy again.

She finally barreled through door a minute later, her expression determined.

Noah gave her a helpless look I'd never seen from him before.

"Help her. Please."

The timbre of Noah's voice was marked by a helplessness I'd never heard before.

"Out of the way," she said to Noah without heat. "I need to assess."

He moved to my other side while Kimmy dropped next to me.

"Apply pressure around the wound," she said, "but be careful not to push the arrow deeper. I need my kit."

"Where's John?" Noah asked.

"Keeping watch outside. We saw what happened."

She opened her bag while Noah pressed hard against my wound. Pain shot through my whole body, and I screamed.

"Kimmy," Noah growled. "Hurry. She's in pain."

"Yeah, no shit," she shot back, pulling scissors out of her medical kit. "I'm going as fast as I can, so shut up and let me work."

She cut through my shirt to look at the wound. Noah grabbed my right hand with both of his and held it in his lap. I'd never seen his face so twisted with fear.

"It's deep," Kimmy muttered. "I don't feel confident removing it here. Risk of infection is too high."

"So what, then?" Noah asked, sounding desperate. "We can't just leave it in!"

"Right now, that arrow is stopping her from bleeding out," she replied grimly. "She needs surgery. We'll have to take her to the clinic."

Panic gripped me. I'd never make it back. Not like this.

"Kim," I whispered, my voice thin. "Am I going to die?"

"No, kitten," Noah said before Kimmy could answer, and he stroked my hair. "You'll be alright. We just gotta get you home."

But the awful tremor in his voice gave him away. He didn't believe it. Not really.

“I’m gonna need to cut this arrow down before we move her,” Kimmy said. “Bolt cutters.”

She held out her hand and Noah gave her the bolt cutters from his pack. I shut my eyes. Noah held my hand as Kimmy trimmed the arrow. The pain was horrible, blinding, and I shut my eyes.

“It’s okay,” Noah kept murmuring to me. “I’m here. I won’t let you go.”

The pain and shock were pulling me under. Letting go felt like a relief, and I gave in and passed out.

Things came in pieces from there, jumbled and disconnected. Noah carrying me over his shoulder to Kimmy’s horse. The steady sound of hoofbeats on the ride home, laid over the saddle like a sack of grain. But the worst part was the piercing agony of the surgery.

I didn’t remember being laid on the exam table, but it would be hard to forget the searing pain of Kimmy and her grandmother carefully working the arrowhead out of my wound with forceps. I screamed and struggled, but Noah and John and Oisín were suddenly there, holding me down. Half-crazy, I sobbed against the cold metal of the table and babbled at them. Begged Noah to help me.

The last thing I remembered was the unexpected touch of his lips on my forehead, and his deep voice soothing me with words I didn’t understand.

Chapter 6

Isla

"I'm sorry," a hoarse voice whispered. "So sorry, darlin'."

It sounded like Noah. But that didn't seem right, because he was obviously crying, and I hadn't seen Noah cry since we were eight and I fell and broke my ankle while we were playing. He'd half-dragged, half-carried me back to my house, crying every time I did from the pain.

His uneven breath continued, and I felt something wet on my hand. A teardrop.

"You have to pull through for me, Isla," he said shakily. "I'll be a mess without you."

"You're right," I mumbled without opening my eyes, feeling like I had a mouth full of sawdust. "Who will annoy you without me?"

"God," he murmured, swiping at his eye before clasping my hand in both of his. "So glad you're awake. How you feeling?"

My shoulder had a deep, slow-burning ache that meant whatever damage was done wasn't just surface-level.

"Like hot garbage," I replied, feeling sluggish. "Worse than that time we rode our bikes off the top of the hill behind Brookside and I got a concussion."

"That bad, huh? I seem to remember that being your idea, too."

I opened one eye. "You just here to lecture me on my bad life decisions? Because if so, I'm way ahead of you."

He sobered. "No. I'm just glad you're still with us. I was...real scared there, for a minute."

His hands were warm and rough with calluses—just like I remembered. Just his presence—his oversized body comically stuffed into a way-too-small chair at my bedside—comforted me. But he'd also ignored me for weeks, and I couldn't pretend that didn't still hurt.

"Really?" I huffed. "Funny way of showing it, the way you've been these last few weeks."

"I know," he replied, the corners of his mouth turning down. "I was a complete idiot, and I'm so sorry. You know how I get."

I snorted. "Yeah, shut down as soon as feelings get involved."

"I know," he said again. "I'm a regular ass. If it helps...I think I lost my mind a little."

I sighed. "I don't think you did—at least not at first. It *was* wrong of me to treat you as my fallback guy, even though I didn't mean to. That night we had together...it made me see things totally differently."

Noah shook his head. “It still wasn’t right, freezing you out, making you think I didn’t want you anymore...when the truth was, I’d never wanted you more. You gave me a taste of you. A night of what I’d wanted for as long as I could remember, and I guess...I was scared.”

I softened a little at his unhappy expression.

“Why?”

He gave a gruff, humourless laugh. “Because I wanted all of you. After that, I couldn’t be happy with anything less anymore. And I’d convinced myself that you’d go back to John after, and I was jealous as all hell, and I couldn’t stand the thought of watching you with him again after I’d come so close to having you for myself.”

I swallowed. “I thought...I thought you pushed me away because you didn’t want me after all.”

He scoffed. “Kitten, I’ve wanted you since I was old enough to know what that meant. You’re the one who’s been with me through everything, including my own stupidity around social stuff. You’re the only one who cared to...know me for real.”

“You’re not stupid,” I said softly, squeezing his hand.

“Well, I am, because it took almost losing you forever to make me realize that I don’t care if I’m your second choice—I need you,” he replied, his voice dropping almost to a whisper. “It’s always been you, Isla. I love you. I want our future. Just give me another chance to treat you right.”

My eyes burned, and my shoulder gave another painful twinge. I opened my mouth to answer, but the door to the back room opened and Kimmy entered.

"How's it going?" she asked sympathetically, then shot Noah an irritable look. "You were supposed to get me when she woke up, Noah."

He shrugged, and Kimmy sat on my bedside to check my vitals and examine my shoulder. I cried a little when she gently moved it back and forth in the socket, testing its range of motion. Noah kissed the palm of my hand and stroked my forehead in soothing circles, his face lined with worry.

"All things considered, could've been worse," she said to me. "But infection's still a concern, and you're on bedrest for at least a week. After the wound closes, we'll try some physiotherapy to improve the range of motion. But no riding, no farmwork, nothing that'll stop that wound from healing, until we give you the all-clear."

I'd hate that, but I nodded along as she gave us instructions for changing the dressings. Finally, she gave me with some pain medicine, which I desperately needed, and left again, with a sharp glance at Noah.

"No upsetting her," she said on her way out. "She needs rest."

The door shut, and I rolled my eyes. "Sorry. She's a little protective."

"Don't blame her. I'd feel the same if someone hurt you."

There was a long, easy silence between us—just the way it used to be—and I started to get sleepy from the medicine.

"Noah," I mumbled.

"Yeah, kitten?"

"I love you too," I said. "Just wanted you to know."

I groaned as I tried to sit up, only for him to abruptly push me back down with one large hand on my good shoulder.

"You shouldn't move," he said, scolding but still gentle. "Getting you to stay still and heal is gonna be harder than teaching a fish to climb, isn't it?"

"I wanted to kiss you," I confessed sheepishly.

He gave me one of his rare smiles. "Is that all? Let me come to you, then."

Noah sat on the edge of the bed and enveloped my hand in his, holding it against his chest as he leaned down and pressed his lips to mine. It was soft and sweet, just like our first kiss, but there was an undercurrent of need and longing in it that excited me. I let out a tiny moan as he parted my lips with his tongue. His lips were warm and sure. His body was relaxed, and he kissed me with his whole heart now.

When we broke apart, I pulled him back down by his t-shirt for more.

Noah chuckled, and said in a low, intimate voice, "That's enough for now, darlin'. We'll kiss plenty later. In fact, it's probably the only way I'll be able to keep you still while you heal up."

I grinned. "I can think of another way that doesn't involve me even getting off my back."

"I'm sure you can," he said, amused. "But we won't be having that kind of fun for a while yet. Rest; I'll be here."

I closed my eyes and let myself drift at last, Noah's hand still covering mine on the bed.

***

Over the next few days, I became convinced that recovery was just another word for torture.

Thanks to Kimmy and the rest of the medical staff's careful attention, I'd avoided infection, but that didn't mean that healing was easy. Even after the wound closed, my shoulder was still damaged internally, and though Kimmy was ever the optimist, Aoife told me the truth: it'd likely never be quite the same.

"We'll cross that bridge," Noah said every time I brought it up, and I let him hold me close, savouring the *we* in that statement. Whatever happened, I wouldn't be handling it alone.

He seemed to be making up for lost time, because in those few days, when pretty much the only thing I was accomplishing was sleeping and hanging around in bed, all he did was fuss over me. Was my pillow fluffed enough? Was I hungry? Did I need more water? Why was I lying differently—was my shoulder hurting too much?

It was cute for a while, until I started getting irritated with being treated like an invalid. I finally told him that if he didn't stop, I'd give him a smack... with my bad arm. Which, of course, only made him chuckle in that deep, quiet way of his, charming me into kissing him. Dick. He knew he was my weakness.

Physiotherapy was agony in the beginning, and the only thing that got me through it was that Noah was there for every session. He encouraged me, held me when I cried from the pain, and always brought fresh-baked cookies and apple cider, direct from the orchard at Brookside. It was impossible not to love a guy who fed me, and the makeout sessions after physio didn't hurt, either.

In the evenings, when I was fed up with lying around all day, Noah kept me busy with chatter, cuddling, and eventually, *finally,* sex.

"Come on, Noah," I begged one afternoon, tangled with him on his bed after an intense makeout session. My shoulder was bound with bandages again to hold it still. "I'm fucking dying over here. Please. I want you so bad.

You can't give me the best night of my life and then refuse to give me more."

"I don't want to hurt you," he said, kissing me ever so gently. "But I want you too."

I used my good arm to feel over his body through his clothes, and he let out a short breath. I sought out the shape of his cock, hard beneath his pants, and stroked. He groaned.

"That's not gonna work," he gasped out.

"Really? 'Cause it really seems like it's working."

Noah snorted, then caught my wrist to stop me. "If I give you some, will you promise to take a nap this afternoon? I'm talking in bed, with pillows and blankets, for more than fifteen minutes."

"Psh, deal," I scoffed. "Easiest bargain ever."

"We'll see, since so far, you hate resting."

Noah levered himself up over me, careful not to put any of his weight on me.

"Stay still and relax," he murmured, his gaze soft as it traveled down my body. "No moving. Promise?"

I exhaled slowly on his neck, enjoying the possessive look in his eyes. "I promise."

"Good."

He lowered his lips to my neck and kissed a line onto my jaw. I sighed. His beard tickled my cheek as he bent to kiss my mouth, gently pressing his tongue past my lips. I tensed a little and was rewarded with a sharp pang in my shoulder, making me gasp against Noah's lips.

"I heard that," he said. "Stop tensing up."

"Not like I meant to," I mumbled irritably.

He smiled a little at my crabbiness. "I know. But them's the rules. So if you don't want me to stop, you'll try a bit harder."

He cut off my retort with another kiss, and I quickly forgot anything but his tongue tangling with mine and the way he slowly slipped his hand into my shirt. He cupped my breast as he kissed me, toying with me by stroking my nipple through the fabric of my bra. I had to make a conscious effort not to tense against him, but I let myself moan into his mouth.

"That's it," Noah murmured as he pulled back to look at my face. "Close your eyes for me. Just feel it."

I let my eyelids flutter closed, and he took the opportunity to carefully lift my shirt and spread kisses onto my belly. Surprised, I giggled, then sighed as he made him way back up toward my breasts. He lifted my bralette over them, giving himself access, then flicked my nipple with his tongue. A thread of pleasure shot straight to my pussy.

"Noah," I whined. "Don't tease me."

He kissed around my nipple. "Sorry, it's just...never gonna get tired of hearing you moan my name, kitten."

I willed my body to stay totally relaxed and boneless as he unbuttoned my pants and slid them to my knees along with my underwear. I opened my eyes as he spread my legs and watched his mouth dip between my thighs. He kissed the tuft of hair there, and I tensed in response, only to whimper when my shoulder gave me shit for it.

"Breathe, darlin'," Noah said, trailing his lips across my thigh.

I did as he said, breathing slowly and deeply through my nose, and then closed my eyes again. He teased me just a bit more, kissing my inner thighs, and I wanted to scream with impatience...until he gave my clit a slow, cautious lick, testing me out. A low moan rolled across my lips, deep and uncontrolled.

That little sound, edged with pent-up need, was all it took, apparently.

He grabbed my hips and buried his face between my thighs. He licked me messily, with no real pattern or plan—just raw, unhinged need. I gave a little cry at the sudden pleasure and forced myself to stay loose and relaxed, even as Noah ate me out like I was the best thing he'd ever tasted, pinning my thighs to the bed.

"Noah," I whimpered. "Oh, God, please."

He slipped two fingers into my wet, aching pussy and fucked me with them—too slowly, too carefully, not enough for me. I tensed my thighs, but caught myself before I hurt myself again.

"That's it," Noah said softly, still fucking his fingers in and out of me. "I'm makin' you feel real good, huh?"

His slight Southern twang always seemed to come out more when he was out of control, and I loved it. It turned me on even more, knowing he was watching me and enjoying it.

"Yeah," I managed to get out. "Oh, yeah."

"So good. You think you can come for me, kitten?"

"Yeah," I gasped. "Oh, fuck, Noah, I'm gonna come."

In response, he sucked hard on my clit, and I exploded. Screamed like I'd never heard myself scream before. An orgasm so intense that even the pain in my shoulder momentarily retreated.

I lay there, limp and totally satisfied, as Noah kissed me and went to his bathroom to clean up. By the time he came back, I had a plan.

"Let me touch you," I said in a low voice, reaching into his pants and finding his half-hardened cock using my good arm.

"That's...not a good idea," he gritted out, but he didn't pull away.

"Your cock seems to think it's a great idea."

That got a clipped laugh out of him. "Yeah, but...your shoulder—"

"You won't hurt me," I soothed. "See? I'm using my good hand. Please, Noah? I want to make you come, too."

He made a guttural, feral sort of sound, then surrendered. Lay back and opened his pants, letting me get my hand fully around his substantial cock. I stroked him in rhythm, then moved to play gently with his balls. He shuddered, but he didn't take his eyes off me.

He held my eyes with his as I stroked him closer and closer. There was something super hot about the intense eye contact he held with me right until the end.

"I love you," he gasped, at the edge. "Oh, God, Isla."

He groaned loudly and I sighed as he covered my hand with milky ropes of come.

"You're gonna ruin me, darlin'," Noah panted as we lay in the afterglow. "It's hard enough knowing I can't make love to you without hurting you, when it's all I want to do every day. It's another thing when you touch me like that and fill my head with such dirty thoughts."

I giggled. "What *kind* of dirty thoughts?"

"Wouldn't you love to know?" he replied wryly, before getting up to fetch a towel.

"Yeah, I would."

"Soon," he promised, wiping my hand clean. "When you're better. I got a whole night planned for us."

"Good," I said, giving him a kiss as he settled in with me for a well-deserved afternoon nap. "Because I've got a whole life planned for us."

Epilogue

Noah

OCTOBER 2097

FOUR YEARS LATER

"Gimme that, kitten," I said, exasperated. "You know you're not meant to be working right now. I turn my back for one minute..."

I took the rake from her. I'd gone to get a ladder to clear the gutters on the farmhouse, and here she was, doing work she wasn't supposed to for the hundredth time.

"I'm pregnant, not a child," Isla said, irritated. "I can do some work."

"Like hell you can," I shot back. "Ain't you supposed to let your husband do all the work now? Thought you'd be happy for the break."

She huffed in a catlike way, earning her nickname. I couldn't help smiling. Reluctantly, she took a seat on the garden bench in front of the house, rubbing her giant belly. She'd barely been showing until a couple weeks ago. As soon as she hit the eight-month mark, her belly ballooned practically overnight.

"Happy? I'm bored to tears," she said miserably. "Can't ride, can't scav, can't even rake the damn leaves because my husband treats me like a delicate flower."

I rolled my eyes and leaned the rake up against the side of the house. "How come the way you say it, it sounds like an insult? Delicate flowers are beautiful."

I walked to the bench and stooped to give my grumpy little wife a kiss. She sighed and wrapped her arms around my neck. She smelled like apples from the orchard; we'd been picking earlier that day. Or, more accurately, I'd made her watch while I picked them, even as she protested.

I may have been overprotective...but I couldn't make myself care. She was my whole world, and she was carrying my baby. We'd suffered a loss once before, and now that we were so close, nothing was going to stop us from having the family I knew she'd always wanted. She and our sweet babe inside her were what I lived for these days.

"Sorry," she said softly as we broke apart. "I'm just ready for the baby to get here."

"Me too," I replied, tucking a stray lock of golden hair behind her ear. "But it's not long now. Let me finish up out here and then we can work inside, okay?"

Isla nodded and didn't complain even once while I finished the gutters, which were full to bursting now that it was fall. Some people probably wondered why we even bothered tending to what they now saw as an empty, abandoned farmhouse, but...we still had hope. Even two years on, we had hope.

Living in the Valley meant you had to believe in people's ability to bounce back, because without it, we'd never have survived.

"Let's head on in," I finally said to Isla. "I'll even let you do some sweeping."

"Such a gentleman," she said sarcastically, but her pretty lips were turned up at the corners in amusement.

"Sure am trying to be, despite my wife's insistence that she do everything herself, even though she's about to pop."

She laughed and waved me through the front door. As promised, I let her do the sweeping while I took inventory of the house, making sure nothing was missing. Thankfully, everything was in order, just like last time.

"You done?" I asked Isla as I came down the stairs from the second floor.

She didn't answer right away. When I looked to her, she was staring out the grimy glass of the back door, looking out at Summerhurst's barren homestead. Red and gold leaves blew across the landscape, and the overcast sky made the picture seem gloomy.

"You alright?" I said, a little worried about her silence. "Your shoulder bugging you?"

Though healed from the incident four years ago, Isla's shoulder had never been quite the same since. She had flares of chronic pain now, especially in these cooler temps. She'd gone through a short period of grief for it, but spirited as she was, she got used to it soon enough, and trained in physiotherapy until she could do everything just like she used to.

"You think they'll come back?" she said softly, and the sudden vulnerability in her voice made me ache. "You think they're alright out there?"

I made it over to her in two strides and took her into my arms.

"Of course they are, darlin'," I murmured, stroking her hair. "Not easy, what they left to do. Dangerous and time-consuming. But if there's a way for anyone to make it back, you know Kimmy and John'll be the ones to do it. Knowing John, he'll probably bring back a case of them."

Truth was, nobody knew if they were even alive, and a lot of the Valley had written them off as dead already. They'd been gone nearly two years, after all, and only their friends kept the house from totally falling into disrepair. But I'd seen them in action when those maneaters attacked us four years ago. I'd seen Kimmy nurse Isla back from the brink. And something deep inside me said they were still out there somewhere. What they'd found, and what they'd bring home with them, was a different question.

"What if they don't?" Isla whispered. "Or what if they're too late? They installed the last of the spares a month ago. If they don't find the PNCs—"

I held her at arm's length so I could meet her eye, then gave her a firm kiss.

"They'll come back," I said with conviction. "And even if they were too late, we'll figure it out, just like we have everything else."

"But the baby—"

I stroked her belly. "Will be fine. He'll have us, either way."

Isla sighed. "Wish Kimmy was here to deliver him."

"I know, kitten. But then you'll get to introduce him to her."

She smiled. "True. I love you, you know. Somehow, you always seem to know what to say."

"Easy to know with my desert island girl."

Hand-in-hand, we made our way back out to our little horse-drawn buggy, setting a course for home—together, as we'd always been from the beginning and would be till the end.

About the Author

E.S. Luck is a copywriter by day and an author when no one is watching. She enjoys reading, writing genre-bending fiction, and extolling the virtues of grammar, much to the collective dismay of all who meet her. She owns too much makeup and lives in Ontario with her husband and their adorable dog, Rosie. *Island* is a prequel novella to her debut post-apocalyptic romance novel, *The Wastelander.*

Visit her online at esluckauthor.com.

Also by E.S. Luck

The Old World is dead. Alone and starving, her only salvation is him.

This steamy post-apocalyptic romance follows Claire Ainsley, a resident of a secure compound isolated from the outside world, as she's unexpectedly thrown out into the brutal post-apocalyptic landscape that compound dwellers call the Wasteland.

With no survival skills, she's captured by the cannibalistic Wastelanders she's always feared. She's rescued by John Madigan, a strong and capable survivor—and a Wastelander. He teaches Claire to survive, and eventually, neither can resist the blazing passion between them. However, with John's personal mission ending and unknown dangers lurking around every corner, Claire may have to learn to survive without the man who's become her only lifeline in a fallen world.

www.ingramcontent.com/pod-product-compliance
Lightning Source LLC
Chambersburg PA
CBHW060611310726
48982CB00003B/521

* 9 7 8 1 7 3 8 3 1 2 2 3 8 *